THE CARRIAGE STONE

SIGBJØRN HØLMEBAKK (1922-1981) was born near Flekkefjord in Southern Norway, where his ancestors had been farmers for generations. He was one of nine children, of which the two eldest were born in the United States, where his father served for many years as a minister in congregations of Scandinavian immigrants.

The author spent most of his adult years in Oslo. After attending a business school and working at various jobs, he became an employee of the State Directorate of Enemy Property, where he was employed for five years.

He left a rich body of work. Prominent are *The Fimbul Winter*, *The Maiden's Leap* and *Twelve Men from Trøndelag and Two Other Stories*. His fiction has been translated into many languages, but this is the first English translation of *The Carriage Stone*. It was awarded the Norwegian Literary Critics' prize in 1975, the year in which it was published. The novel was also a popular Norwegian Book Club choice and later became a well-known film abroad.

Hølmebakk's first book was a collection of short stories (1950), followed by another book of stories and eight novels. His novels, Jentespranget *(The Maiden's Leap)*, Fimbulvinteren *(The Fimbul Winter)*, and Hurra for Andersens *(Hurrah for Andersens)*, were successful films abroad, as was *Salve, The Shepherd*, a children's film. His essays and prose writings were collected in three volumes, the last volume published posthumously to mark his 70th anniversary.

FRANCES DIEM VARDAMIS, translator, a native of New York City, studied Norwegian at the Foreign Service Institute in Washington, D.C. and at the University of Oslo. She resides in Vermont.

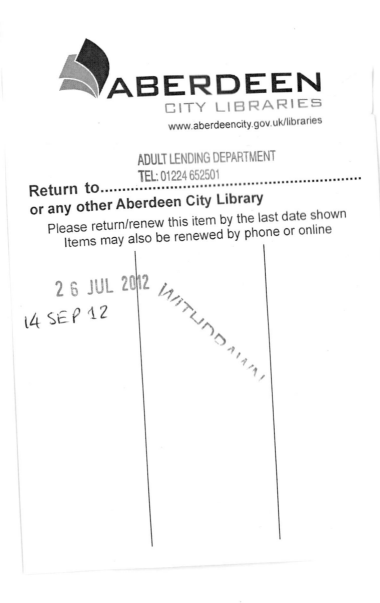

the Carriage Stone.

Sigbjørn Hølmebakk

Translated from the Norwegian
by Frances D. Vardamis

Parthian
The Old Surgery
Napier Street
Cardigan
SA43 1ED

www.parthianbooks.com

Originally published as *Karjolsteinen*
by Sigbjørn Hølmebakk
© Gyldendal Norsk Forlag 1975
All Rights Reserved

Translated from the Norwegian
by Frances D. Vardamis © 1996

ISBN 978-1-905762-28-6

Cover design by theundercard.com
Printed and bound in the United States of America

Published with the financial support of the Welsh Books Council.

Was it mere coincidence?

If he believed in God, he would, perhaps, have said that there was meaning in what happened. But he was a communist and did not believe in higher meaning. Therefore it disturbed him that a chance encounter was wreaking havoc with plans for his work.

On the 2nd of April, Victor, the party secretary, telephoned and asked him to take over as May Day speaker at a rally near Kristiansand. The party member who originally had been assigned the address, unexpectedly had to travel with a delegation to East Berlin. Olav Klungland immediately replied that it was impossible. He was in the middle of work on a novel that was supposed to be out in the autumn, and if the manuscript was not delivered by the first of August, the publication would be delayed for over a year. Besides, he had to be at a writers' conference in Stockholm in the middle of April. But Victor kept pressing, probably because he knew that his arguments would get results. Klungland ought to give this speech — there could be political repercussions if he said no. It was a reciprocal arrangement with various left wing groups — one of the few such meetings in the country. There had been a hotly contested vote in the local general committee, and, with a plurality of only two votes, it was necessary that someone from the party give the main address. All the usual speakers were busy, and it would be a political setback if they now had to send regrets.

Finally Klungland said yes, and went immediately to work on a rough draft in order to have the speech out of the way before his trip to Stockholm. When, two days later, he telephoned the party office to ask them to send him some brochures containing information he needed, Victor asked him to drive out to the Radium Hospital and visit an old political associate who had been admitted for a third time. This time, as well, he said no at first. The patient was an older man whom he knew only casually, the way political associates know each other. They had run into each other at meetings and rallies; on one occasion they were members of the same committee. Klungland used the May Day speech he had to deliver as an excuse.

"I'm so sorry, but I'm right in the middle of work on this speech...," he began. But as soon as he had spoken he felt guilty, and he knew that when he put the receiver down he would regret his refusal. He judged himself, as if from the perspective of an outsider. Here he was, sitting comfortably at his desk in his fine house and refusing to visit a terminally ill comrade who from his earliest youth had fought for the cause.

"He would appreciate your coming. He's all alone, you know, and no one visits him. Even I don't have time...."

"I know that, but..."

"And you have plenty of time before your speech. You don't have to be with him more than half an hour."

"I'll do it in a few days," Klungland responded tersely, but, realizing the annoyance in his tone, he added, "Of course, I'll be glad to do it. Is there anything I can bring along for him?"

"I don't think he needs anything anymore. Only a visit."

It irritated Klungland to be reminded of how much time he had. Was that because he knew that he did not use his hours wisely? He had begun work on the novel two years before, but he had gotten nowhere. Last fall he began in earnest, and he would have finished it by now, had he used his time well. But he could not endure sitting at his desk for days and even weeks without accomplishing anything. It made him feel unpleasantly useless, as if his work were mere folly, a weary groping through a fog in which he neither knew where he had come from nor where he wanted to go. "Write anything that comes into your head just so that you get going, and you can revise it later," Vigdis would say when she noticed that he was cross and despondent after yet one more unsuccessful day. But what should he write about? The words did not come; the language would not work right. His work was nothing but scribbled paper and confusion and illegible notes. Inevitably, when that happened, he would abandon his writing and tackle something real. He would be enormously relieved to be doing something tangible. Mornings he would awaken joyful, knowing the day's work was concrete and finite. He had decided to replace the siding on his house. In the fall he had assembled all his material and had drawn up a strict schedule: from nine to two he would write, and afterwards he would work on the house. However, just as he had foreseen, he stuck to his plan for only a few days. All his struggles at his desk, all his abortive attempts that seemed so unpleasant because they were so unreal, vanished like mist on a summer morning. He let himself be completely absorbed in his task: the boards, the blows of the hammer, the insulation and the complicated window frames. And the project succeeded beyond all expectation; better than he had dared to hope. Each evening in the gathering dusk he would stroll out to the garden and admire what he had done in the course of the day, and, to deaden his guilty conscience, he would calculate what it would have cost if he had hired a builder to do the job. By Christmas the house was finished, and in January he returned to the novel. He had forgotten it so completely that he had to force himself to recall what, in fact, he had wanted to write about. But slowly, painfully slowly, he got back into the rhythm of writing. Eventually, he became so absorbed that Vigdis would have to call him repeatedly for meals. And when he went to bed in the evening — he retired early and denied himself the drink that was his usual indulgence — he placed a pad and pencil on his desk because he knew that, in the moment of waking, a sentence or a solution to a problem might clarify itself. It was a question of writing it down before it vanished. Without his knowing how it happened, the plot — or, at least, the outline of the plot — began to take shape and the characters began to assume a kind of living reality. He decided to remain at their cottage after the Easter holidays to work on the book.

And then, in the middle of all this, Victor called about the May Day speech. After Klungland worked on the speech for a week — reading the papers and news magazines, perusing old manuscripts of other speeches, calling party comrades — he began to find an approach, and he noticed that thing happening which, all along, he knew would happen: everything that he had worked on in the last months became lifeless. When he tried to think about the characters that had so thoroughly occupied his imagination some days before, he realized, with a sense of shame, that in creating them he had, to a degree, distanced himself from the world of reality. If only he could combine his creative writing with political engagement; if only he had the ability to write the kind of political literature that the young writers these days turned out and that he quite honestly envied, he would not have this conflict. He had tried, but he could not manage it. Each time, he realized that what he wanted to say could be better expressed in a lecture or through political action. Each time his attempts at writing ended in despair.

He had gradually come to terms with his problem. Now, once more, he realized a deep contentment. He was working with the concrete reality of the speech. His theme sought him out constantly, in the radio news and in newspaper headlines — suffering, want, exploitation, brutal displays of power. Growing out of his excitement, the sentences formed themselves almost without resistance. Even the trivial inspired him, because he knew it could be overcome through engagement and struggle. And solidarity. That was what the speech should be about.

For years the left had been powerless because of internal dissension. Despairing, he had seen insignifi-

cant squabbles, suspicions, and egoism poison relation-
ships among socialists who, in reality, were fighting for
the same goals. For years he had spoken and written in
hope of breaking this vicious circle — a long and more
or less hopeless struggle, which often had ended in
attacks on friends. Now he was on the verge of victory.

"I can talk with him about this," he thought, as he
drove out to the Radium Hospital some days later. The
colleague's name was Jens Heimdal, and Klungland
knew him, as a matter of fact, better than he had at first
thought. Heimdal, too, had been a tireless champion of
solidarity. The few times they had met he had spoken of
almost nothing else. He was one of those hard workers
one could always depend upon, who never said no
when asked to take on extra work. All of his free time
went to political work, to demonstrations, rallies, union
meetings (he was a carpenter), and he was always hur-
rying from mailbox to mailbox with newspapers, brochures, and pamphlets. Heimdal continued his efforts
even after he became ill. He worked quietly. When he
talked with people he was always calm and friendly. He
never let himself be provoked. Heimdal belonged to that
older generation that many on the left used as an argument against cooperation. "Now look here," they would
say, "with whom are we actually supposed to be cooperating? Aren't you talking, by and large, about that
bunch of old fogies who don't know whether they're
coming or going?"

Olav Klungland was always furious when he heard
that argument, particularly coming from those who had
stayed safely away from politics in the days when there
was a real price to pay for working for the party and who

now rode into the left on the current wave of popularity for radical causes. They came into the movement too easily and therefore, in less than a year, they were free of all doubt and of all middle class convention. He listened to their predictable contributions to the debates — they were revolutionaries without stain or blemish, without temptation; now and then he had to doubt his own revolutionary zeal when he listened to them.

That was what he wanted to tell Jens Heimdal. Simply put, he wanted to thank him for his contribution and assure him that it had not been in vain.

But once he entered the main waiting room at the Radium Hospital, he began to wonder if that would be the right thing to say. It would sound, after all, like a eulogy; it might shock Heimdal, reminding him, as it would, of the seriousness of his condition. People usually expressed that kind of gratitude only about the dead. In any case, Klungland did not get to see Heimdal immediately. It would be a half hour before the patient could receive visitors, the receptionist said. (Later he learned that Heimdal was just then receiving a blood transfusion.)

He waited over an hour, and later, when he thought back on it, he was not sure if the time went quickly or slowly. Often he thought the clock had stopped; when he looked at the hands, they seemed hardly to have moved. But when he brought his watch to his ear he heard the quiet ticking, and the sound filled him with an inexplicable anxiety. He vacantly listened to the sharp female voice that came over the loudspeaker calling people, by number, to the outpatient clinic: "Red, number 41; black, number 18." Each time, someone would get up and disappear into one of the side rooms that invariably had a mirror on the back wall. To stop thinking, he tried to read, but then, each time the woman's voice rang over the loudspeaker, he could not resist looking up from his newspaper to see who was summoned.

When he first arrived, he had been rather surprised to see so many in the waiting room. Did all of these people really have cancer? They sat and read magazines, looked at the clock, or knitted. In front of the newspaper kiosk there was a line, and in the cafeteria there was another line. It was the ordinary, the everyday that disturbed him — it was like the waiting room of an airport. Later it dawned on him that it was precisely on that point that his anxiety began in earnest: the connection with an airport, and then the voice that continually called up new numbers, always followed by someone who stood up and disappeared behind a door.

He began to observe his surroundings more carefully, and new details presented themselves. In a niche in the corner of the hall there was a fountain with a colored plastic ball that danced round and round in the jet of water. Nearby were small tables where people sat and drank coffee.

What was most upsetting was the apparently carefree mood that reigned in this tastefully decorated waiting room. A shabby room would have been better. Efficient nurses — they all wore some sort of medal on their uniforms — came and went, and when they met patients they knew, they stopped and inquired about their health; they were cheerful and optimistic, as if they were discussing a cold. Two doctors were in conversation in a corner. They apparently were telling jokes or gossiping about a colleague who had behaved foolishly, and one of them slapped his thigh and laughed aloud before he walked off. He passed right by Olav Klungland. The doctor's face was red with suppressed mirth. Strange, Klungland thought, in this house of death.

To avoid sitting idly by, Klungland walked over and joined the cafeteria line. The friendly, heavyset woman behind the counter chatted and laughed as she served, and when it was his turn, she stood with coffee pot in hand and stared across the hall. "Look," she said.

A man stood there studying a painting. He wore an elegant royal blue dressing gown over his hospital clothing, and at that moment, he pushed both hands in the pockets of his gown and walked on with a quick, light step. It was obvious that he realized he was being observed. When the man passed a row of columns at the end of the hall, it seemed he no longer bothered with his pretense. His shoulders slumped forward and he shuffled off with a tired step.

The man was a well-known actor. Olav Klungland had met him many years before when the actor had played a minor role in a film for which Klungland had written the script. As the actor disappeared behind the columns he glanced over without recognizing Klungland. The actor's face was sickly pale and on his thin neck, marks, like a picture frame, had been drawn in black ink.

The year before, Klungland had seen him on the stage. He and Vigdis had been celebrating the arrival of a royalty payment for a repeat performance of a play on Radio Theater. They had been delighted because the money had been so unexpected, and they drank two glasses of sherry at the bar. Klungland no longer recalled the name of the play or what it was about, but he remembered their festive mood as they sat in the darkness and waited for the curtain to rise. The actor, whom he now saw disappear among the columns, had played a dynamic business man, and Klungland remembered the fresh, tan face and the radiant blue eyes that sparkled in the spotlights

Just then, the nurse came and told Klungland that she would take him up to Jens Heimdal.

It was a short visit, perhaps fifteen minutes, perhaps less, not because he could not bring himself to stay longer, but because he felt that there was nothing he could do there. There was nothing he could say or do that could help or comfort. The man who lay in bed needed no comfort, and, it dawned on Klungland, neither did he want it. But what did he need? What did he want? Klungland was unprepared for that question and it struck him like an ice-cold wind.

While Klungland hesitated, standing by the bed, the nurse straightened the blanket and spoke soothingly to her patient, telling him that he had a visitor, that it was always nice to have a visitor. She spoke as if to an infant. When, with a smile, she disappeared through the door, Klungland was suddenly afraid of being alone with the emaciated, deathly-pale sick man who lay with half-closed eyes. When Heimdal recognized Klungland, he nodded weakly, but he continued to stare into space. There was something distant and terrifying in the gaze, and Klungland began to think about the death scene in his last novel. It had been difficult to write, but in the reviews the critics had stressed precisely that scene; they praised it as an uncompromisingly realistic portrayal of the inevitable. Now he understood how false it was; it was as unreal as the memory of the actor whose blue eyes glistened in the spotlights.

Later, when Olav Klungland would meet Eilif Grøtteland outside, he would once more be reminded of his novel, but by that time his experience in the hospital would have already become unreal, something from which he would have distanced himself. Now, in the hospital room, he was face to face with a human being who was dying, and he realized that he was unable to meet Heimdal's gaze. He began to search for something in the past that could ease the unpleasantness of looking at the dying man. At last Klungland remembered a district election campaign four years before, an early morning when they stood together near the East Railway Station and passed out pamphlets about contract negotiations. It was nasty and drizzling so that Jens Heimdal had to hold his pile of brochures under his raincoat to keep them dry. He had been alert and watchful that no one should slip past without getting a pamphlet. That time, too, he had watched Heimdal's eyes — and marveled. They were friendly, but hard and persistent. Why did he do it, Klungland had thought. He surely knew that the passersby would not bother to read the pamphlets, and that he, himself, would retire with a pension and enjoy no benefit whatsoever from the salary negotiations. Now he lay here and stared absently into space. In a few days Heimdal's obituary would appear in the party newspaper. Perhaps Klungland would even be asked to write it. And later, when Heimdal would be remembered by his comrades over a coffee and Danish after party meetings, one or the other might remark, "He was a first-rate fellow. We need more like him."

Klungland had brought along three books. They lay on the night table; the one, which he had translated, was a description of the revolution in Cuba. Now he realized how absurd it was to give Heimdal these books, and he thought that, surreptitiously, he would slip them back into his pocket. But just as he was doing so, the dying man looked at him, and because Klungland could not meet his eyes without saying something, he began, despite his earlier decision, to discuss that which they had in common. Yet, with every new sentence, he realized how meaningless his words were. Nevertheless, he kept on talking; he mentioned party comrades they both knew, the May Day plans, and how well the various factions on the left were cooperating recently. Joint May Day celebrations were planned for many places, and for the local election there would be combined lists of candidates in over forty communities.

He was not sure that the sick man understood what he said. But suddenly Heimdal looked up and stared at him. "We've spoken all too little about that," he said calmly.

Klungland was startled because the voice was so clear and sharp. And he was relieved: now they had something to talk about.

"You have, in any case, no reason to reproach yourself," he replied. "If there was anyone who fought for this, it was you...." Before he finished it dawned on him that they were talking about two different things, that what the man meant they had not spoken about was precisely what was happening now: death.

"There was no one to talk to!" The dying man's words came in spurts, and yet, they were clear. "At the same time, it wasn't good form. As if somehow to talk about it was a kind of betrayal." Then he returned to staring straight ahead, and nothing more was said. The nurse came in and began, once more, with her baby talk; Klungland left right after that.

Out in the parking lot he met Eilif Grøtteland. Later it bothered Klungland that he did not catch the name when the man introduced himself, but he was so shaken by the meeting with Heimdal that when he saw a stranger heading over from the taxi stand, he knew he had to pull himself together. He did not dare speak at first. Therefore, he was perhaps more brusque than he meant to be. He continued to fumble with his car keys and did not look up, even when the stranger stopped beside him.

"Excuse me, aren't you...." Klungland merely nodded when his name was mentioned. "What a coincidence that I should run into you just now."

"I don't believe we've met before," Klungland replied coolly and shook the hand that reached towards him. He was relieved that he did not know the man. He opened the car door quickly and bent down to get into the driver's seat.

"No, but we were just talking about you," he heard from behind.

"Who?"

"My wife." The man nodded towards the front entrance to the hospital. "The last thing she asked as I was leaving was that I bring her your latest novel. She's always been so enthusiastic about your books."

At first Klungland thought that the man was begging for a free copy. It happened all the time. Irritated, he was about to respond with a sharp retort — that it was a simple matter, that all he had to do was stop by a bookstore — but there was something about the man that made him pause: a blend of determination and restrained desperation. Therefore he responded, without actually wanting to, "Give me the address and I'll be glad to send you a copy," but immediately he realized he had misinterpreted the stranger's intentions.

"Naturally I'll purchase the book myself! But I thought, since now we've chanced to meet, that you could write a short message. I know that would please her."

This last he said softly, almost inaudibly. He certainly did not intend that Klungland hear it.

"If you're driving downtown?" the man continued. "We could stop by a bookstore. It would take only a minute...."

"Unfortunately, I'm going in another direction. But call me, or send the book in the mail and I'll write something...!" He knew his words must sound like a refusal, but he could not bear thinking about a drive downtown now. Perhaps the man would review the entire history of the wife's illness, or, still worse, talk about Klungland's books, asking what he really meant by this or that. To allay his own feeling of guilt, or perhaps purely out of politeness, Klungland rolled the window down after he started the engine and he called out, "Do ring me up. You'll find the number in the telephone book."

When he pulled out of the parking lot, he caught, in the rearview mirror, a glimpse of a tall figure. The stranger was about sixty, with a thin face and a scattering of gray in his hair. There was nothing unusual, neither in his face nor in his stature.

Thus he met Eilif Grøtteland, totally by accident. It could not have happened at a more inopportune moment.

A framed saying of Che Guevara hung over his desk:

> The only way to solve a problem is to begin
> to work on it. If you need an example, show
> what a man does. Do not talk about what
> he ought to do.

Whenever he was depressed, he would repeat the words half aloud, as a ritual, a formula for picking himself up by the scruff of the neck. He recited it the next morning as he sat at his desk and tried to get underway with his work. But it did not help, and he remained seated, staring at the words and waiting for the telephone to ring. When it finally did ring, towards eleven, he raced down the stairs, afraid that the caller would hang up before he reached the phone.

It was Victor, from party headquarters, who called to tell him that the old man had died during the night. He lost consciousness in the evening and died in his sleep just after midnight. They exchanged expressions of sympathy, agreeing that it was for the best, and concluded that Heimdal had been a first-rate human being. "If only they all were like him!" Victor said, somewhat angrily. His aggressive tone was a kind of tribute, a way of hiding his emotions. Victor recalled several unpleasant episodes Heimdal had endured be-

cause he was a party member and he recalled how
courageously the old man had confronted his antago-
nists.

When Victor learned that Klungland had visited the
evening before, he was sincerely pleased. He, himself,
had not had time; there was a meeting. He spoke of how
alone Heimdal had been; a widower, childless, without
family. The party should arrange the funeral.

"Would you be able to say a few words and lay a
wreath from the party?"

"I'm off to Stockholm," Klungland answered. It was
a valid enough reason to refuse.

"Then perhaps you could write a few lines for the
newspaper? That wouldn't take more than half an hour."

That, too, Klungland had expected, but he could
not come up with an excuse. However, he knew that it
would be impossible for him to write the obituary. "No.
And let's not talk about it anymore."

"Sure, sure. It was only a question. It's all right, you
know," Victor said rather wearily, and he wished Klungland a good trip to Stockholm.

There was nothing else to talk about, nothing else
to consider. Even the harrowing visit to the hospital
receded in importance. His comrade was dead, and
Klungland's reaction was, as always in such cases,
"That's unfortunate, but there's nothing that can be
done about it." He felt relieved, as he always did when
a problem was taken out of his hands.

"I don't have time to be depressed now," he
thought when he returned to his desk. "I have to forget
it!" He repeated the words aloud in order to give them
more weight.

However, he found it was not the dead man he had trouble forgetting, but the man he met afterwards. He remembered the silhouette in the rearview mirror, how it grew smaller and smaller. What had the man said? What had he asked for? A book for his sick wife. It was precisely one of his books that she wanted!

Not that there was anything remarkable about the request. People, especially sick people, read books to while away the hours. Because she was a patient at the Radium Hospital, she probably had cancer. Perhaps her illness was incurable. In any case, she must feel that a death sentence was hanging over her. Why did she want to read his book and not someone else's? He could not deny that the thought disturbed him, but as he always did when his emotions were in question, he tested his feelings to find out whether his anxiety was false or genuine, whether it was something he actually felt, or if, perhaps, it were merely a literary problem he was playing with — material he would be working into his notes.

At least the distress he felt in turning the stranger away was genuine. If he had taken the man with him in the car, the request would have been satisfied and he would have been finished with it. Now he did not even remember the stranger's name. The man was supposed to have telephoned, but he did not call, neither that day nor in the days that followed.

Klungland was certain about that because he stayed at home all those days. He did not even go down to the newsstand to buy a paper. Nor was he in the mood to read newspapers. He dawdled around the house or sat at his desk and stared at the walls or at the bookcase where his eleven books were neatly arranged in the order that he had written them; the last one, on the extreme right, was the thickest. That was the one she had wanted. Perhaps her husband had already bought it; perhaps she lay in bed and read it this very moment. For some reason, that upset him. What, actually, had he written?

He took the novel from the shelf, leafed through it, and read at random. When he had been struggling to finish it, he had not thought about who would be reading it. What had he thought about? In any case not this — that it would be read by someone who was dying.

But he knew that he could not have written differently even if he had considered that. What did she think as she read it? And how did his words affect her — for bad or for good? Did it provide her with an experience that made things easier, or did it merely strengthen the fear she knew when, from time to time, she would lay the book aside and think about what was happening to her? Her husband had asked him to write a greeting. But what could he write? "Merry Death and a Happy New Year!" He had to beware of succumbing to his narcissistic feelings of guilt.

He went down to the kitchen, poured a cup of coffee and gazed out into the garden where the buds of the black currant bushes were already turning pale green. When he walked outside, he left the porch door open in case the telephone rang.

It was a glorious spring day, absolutely still beneath an endlessly blue sky. The sun had melted the snow everywhere except under the pile of garden refuse where there remained a patch of gray, frozen slush. I should cart that trash away, he thought, distracted by a sparrow that, intoxicated with springtime, hopped here and there among the red currant bushes. The bird flitted and fluttered around a plum tree and landed on another bush. Suddenly a dark shadow shot out from behind the rubbish heap; it was so quick that he hardly realized what was happening. The cat made a powerful leap — and missed. Ashamed, it crept off, while the sparrow whirled into the air and, totally unaffected, landed more or less where it had perched when he first noticed it. It had been in mortal danger, a hair's breadth from death. If something like that had happened to me, he thought, I would have been in shock, would have remembered it for the rest of my life, and would have told the story to my children and my grandchildren. We think about death from our childhood to our final moment. Not only when we are in mortal danger, but all our lives we dread that which approaches. And I write about it, create gripping descriptions of it, so that those who are in the midst of it have something to read. "Stop!" he shouted to himself. "That's enough!" He spoke so loudly that he was afraid his neighbor, bending over her rock garden only a few meters away, would hear.

He returned to his desk and began to work on his speech. It was already half finished. He tried to imagine the faces he would be addressing, but saw another face instead. "We never spoke about it, there was no one to talk to, and, somehow, it was not good form." With supreme effort he pushed aside the memory. To get back to work, he used a favorite trick of his. Even Vigdis did not know about it. He shut the window and closed the drapes. Then he began to read the speech aloud. He was even careful to begin with "Comrades" and follow up with a full pause, something he had a tendency to make too short. He was conscious of the strength and emotional depths in his voice and of the fine, short sentences. Did his words ring false or true? He continued, and now he was addressing the skeptics: the academics, and the union members who were often the most pedantic of all.

For many hours he sat at his desk and worked with great intensity. For each section, he rehearsed the speech, the tone of his voice, his hand movements. He continued without pause right up until he heard the children downstairs in the hall.

In the evening he and his family burned brush wood in the garden. The blue smoke, merging with the evening sky, shimmered in a moment of absolute peace. Over by the bonfire stood the three children, two girls and a boy – eleven, nine and seven years old – each with a sausage stuck on a stick. He and Vigdis watched nearby, listening to the quiet that only now and then was broken by distant voices from other gardens. Occasionally they stopped to admire the new paneling on the house; the boards had already begun to weather golden in the March sun. Then the phone rang and he raced for it, but it was only his oldest daughter's girlfriend.

Vigdis could not understand why he was so interested in the telephone; it was not like him. "Why is it suddenly so important?" she asked, studying him searchingly. He had told her about the man he had met outside the Radium Hospital.

He did not want to talk about it with her. The conversation would immediately descend to a professional level — his anxiety, she would explain, masked an easily diagnosed psychological complex. She was a professional psychologist and worked at a children's psychiatric institute. Her first husband and their daughter worked there as well. Her first marriage had been stormy, with harrowing and shocking episodes. Secretly it disturbed him. She had told him most of the story, but perhaps not everything? Her first marriage, which had lasted ten years, ended in a custody battle over her daughter that included bitter, hate-filled accusations on both sides.

But after twelve years the anger had eased, and gradually Vigdis and her first husband became not only colleagues but good friends. When Klungland was at the institute and saw them calmly sitting there at the same table in the dining room together with their daughter, he could not but wonder: was there not, in fact, something immoral and inhuman about the enormous level of tolerance in psychologists? He was reminded of something Somerset Maugham had said about actors — they lack souls and ought to be buried outside the church walls.

Their own marriage, now in its twelfth year, had been stormy as well. It had fluctuated between bitter struggles on the brink of divorce and such pure, idyllic heights as now, when they stood lovingly together, gazing on the youngsters in the garden and smiling. However, the possibility for conflict was never-ending and consistent: her rebellion over his egoistic, domineering manner, and disagreement over raising the children. Recently she had achieved a clear advantage. She had her career and used it — ruthlessly, he thought. She even quoted her colleagues and her first husband as authorities when her quarrels with Klungland were at a crisis. That always infuriated him. Not only because he disagreed with some of their assertions, but because he felt himself personally insulted; he, too, knew a little about what stirred up the labyrinth of the mind. *They* analyzed people; *he* created them! He felt less secure when she blamed him for egocentricity and arrogance, because he knew that her accusations were true. But he also knew that that was only half of the truth; the other half was that she, too, was domineering and self-centered. That was true especially of her relationship towards his work. She was at her job from eight to four-thirty, and she treated her career as something almost holy and inviolable.

Once he had come into the therapy room while she was busy with a patient. Her initial fury was only the prelude to a violent quarrel in which she accused him of a crude lack of consideration. He, for his part, reminded her of the countless times when she had disturbed him in his "therapy room" — while he was in the middle of a sentence or deep within the soul of a human being who was being created, not merely analyzed — a human being who only existed in his imagination. At such a moment she would telephone to ask him to shop, or to race off and pick up the children from the nursery school. Could he phone her and say that she had to pick them up because he was busy? He could not, because she was sheltered by her position, her office hours — she was busy with a client.... "That's out of the question," she shouted indignantly. "You're home. You're your own master. Couldn't you, once, pick up the children." And so began the next round. That quarrel went on almost continuously for a fortnight, interrupted only during the hours she was at her work — because, in arguments as well, her office hours were holy and inviolable. Finally they both were so exhausted that they had to give up. Gradually, and particularly after that period, their relationship improved. The youngsters grew older, and they began to play their roles, too. The good times lasted longer, and now they had gotten along well for a good many months. She attributed his anxiety to a natural restlessness connected with the work he was doing, and he let her labor under that delusion.

One evening some days later, he suddenly remembered the stranger's name. They were in bed making love, and he was thinking about nothing but how good life was for them. "Eilif Grøtteland," he said aloud, and he noticed that her hands were immediately still.

"Your mind must be a thousand miles away," she said, hurt.

"I don't know why the name came to me just now."

"Forget him. Now there's only the two of us."

"Certainly."

But in the end he got up, turned on the light, and, so that he would not forget, jotted the name down on a pad. He looked through the telephone book, as well, but he did not find the name listed.

"Aren't you coming back," she called, and he returned to the bedroom.

They lay awake for a long time and talked, but he realized how clumsy his explanation was. He told her only half-truths about his concern.

"In the morning you can telephone the hospital and get the address. But what in the world do you want? Is there something you want to find out from him?"

He did not know. What was it, in fact, that he wanted to learn? Why did this man continue so to occupy his thoughts that he forgot the speech he was supposed to deliver and the novel he was supposed to finish?

As it turned out he met him many times. After returning home on those evenings when he was together with Grøtteland, he would restlessly anticipate their next meeting. Was he interested in what the man told him because it was good material for his next novel? Was it something that quickened his imagination and that he could use later on?

He refused to believe that that was the only reason, but he knew that it must be one of the reasons. There was, as well, some quality in the man's voice, a seriousness and a desperation, that somehow bound him to Klungland and which always revolved around one single word: faith.

Klungland thought on his wife's question as he sat downstairs in the old mid-town hotel and waited for the receptionist to phone up to Eilif Grøtteland's room and tell him that he had a visitor. It had been simple to get the address; all he had to do was tell the truth — he wanted to deliver a book. At the last minute he had remembered to bring it along so that he had a legitimate excuse. He had also written a few words inside — the date, the greeting, and his name. He had thought to deliver the book, exchange a few words and then leave. But it did not turn out that way. Not that the man forced him to listen. Nor was what he learned there so remarkable. Grøtteland's wife was seriously ill, but there was still hope. She was weak, but ambulatory. She would be undergoing a number of tests. Perhaps there would be an operation. The husband planned to stay in Oslo as long as his wife was in the hospital.

It was some time before Grøtteland said anything about himself, and then what piqued Klungland's curiosity was the revelation that the man had, in the past, been a Lutheran minister. He revealed that only because Olav Klungland asked him, directly, about his occupation. And then, when Klungland asked him why he no longer was a minister, Grøtteland's answer was that he could no longer manage it. Somehow the reply sounded comic, like a middle-aged man's problems with impotence.

"A minister who can't manage it! What was it you couldn't manage? To preach, Eilif?" They had, right from the beginning, been on a first name basis, even though the man was at least fifteen years older.

"Yes, that, too." He nodded slowly as if he had thought the matter over carefully. "Preach. Yes, especially that!"

But Klungland did not find that a satisfactory answer.

"When all is said and done is it, in fact, an occupation?"

"It is an occupation. Naturally it's an occupation. But it's also something else." The man stared into space, his eyes deep and penetrating, his face lean and tanned. "Doesn't it ever happen that you, too, can't manage it? I've wondered about that when I read your books. It seems so easy, so natural."

"Sure, it happens. The difficult thing is to make it seem natural."

"A minister also works with words. He's expected to say something. He's always expected to say something. For every occasion."

"And he should believe in what he says?"

"Yes, he must believe in what he says."

"And you no longer believe?"

"I don't know. It sounds strange, but that's the way it is."

They had been talking about books for almost two hours, and Klungland had already risen to leave when Grøtteland said these words. A knock interrupted them, and the maid arrived with coffee. When Grøtteland had called down the order, he had invited his visitor to stay, but Klungland had refused. Now, however, Klungland sat down and took a cup. The conversation had taken an interesting turn.

"But perhaps you should be off to the hospital?" Klungland asked when they were alone once more.

"No, I have time, and I confess that I would like to talk about it." He smiled, a little embarrassed. "There's no one with whom you can discuss it; it's, somehow, not good form."

Not wanting to reveal that he was stunned by the minister's choice of words, Klungland asked quickly, "How, exactly, did it happen?"

"How did it happen? I don't know that myself. But I can never stop wondering about it. The only thing I'm positive about is that I wish that I believed, and that I wish that I knew whether or not I once did truly believe."

On the following evening Grøtteland repeated the same words. They sat in the same room, in the same chairs. But Grøtteland was more anxious now. He had just come from the hospital and had spoken with the doctor.

"I wish I knew if I ever did believe!" he said earnestly, as if his doubt had something to do with his wife's illness. "Perhaps it's no more than a fantasy, a delusion? I often suspect that. But other times, when I think back on the things that happened, especially when I was a child, I'm absolutely certain that I did believe once, that I was happy because I belonged to God. How else could I have known such joy? Nevertheless, I admit, it is difficult to evoke that past happiness again."

There was nothing of the dreamer or the romantic in Grøtteland's words. On the contrary, he manifested an almost aggressive determination, as if he conducted an endless discussion within himself. He chewed on a toothpick, and when he became excited, he snapped it with his teeth, threw it away and took a new one.

"When I think about how good life used to be!" Grøtteland cried. But then he broke off, as if he immediately rejected his own words. "To think about it, to remember, that's one thing. But to experience it again, so that it has value, so that one can take a stand because of it! To be sure, part of it is terrible, the part that is gone. The hours, the moments of happiness you've known. You can't hold on to them. It's as though you're walking through a forest, and suddenly, quite unexpectedly, something remarkable happens, something unbelievably wonderful – a grouse flutters up and disappears into the underbrush. That happened to me once when I was a boy, by a brook at the bottom of a narrow ravine where I often hid when I wanted to be alone. It was my secret place. And suddenly this grouse shot up in front of me. I froze and stared until it disappeared. I wanted so much to see it again. I believed that in some mystical way it would reappear. I had, after all, seen it only a moment before. A moment? That moment was gone forever. And in precisely the same way, one gazes after the grouse that is gone, after the moments that have vanished. One does not believe that they are gone; one believes it is a lie."

"Forgive me," he said and threw one toothpick in the ashtray but immediately reached for another. "As a matter of fact, I'm no longer so concerned about why I gave up the ministry; I know, more or less, the reason. But I wonder more and more often why I ever entered the church, why I made that particular choice. Because, despite everything, it is something one chooses."

He laughed, and briefly he was silent. "Something *I* chose. Why are we so afraid to use that particular word? Why do we feel so ashamed to use the word 'I'? I noticed that yesterday evening when I was reading through some of my old sermons. I don't know why I brought them along. But in any case, I noticed, with surprise, that I had only used words like 'one,' 'we', 'us', 'you' — except when I was ordained.

"It was strange to read that particular sermon again. It seemed so terribly false. In one place I had written, and the words were underlined in the manuscript, 'Ever since I was a little boy, yes, so long as I can remember, Jesus Christ has been the driving force in my life, the spiritual soil from which I drew nourishment.' I found it almost unbelievable that I had written that. About my parents I wrote, 'My mother was a god-fearing, hard-working woman who struggled for her many children. My father suffered from poor health and became disabled at an early age.'

"Why didn't I tell the truth? Why didn't I talk about the terrible suffering he endured, the fear he must have known, the shame...? Was it because that would have shaken the fine people below me in the pews? I'm still moved by an inexplicable anger when I recall those faces. It's inexplicable, because I have no reason to be angry with them. I was the one who was not telling the truth.

"What truth? What I said was true enough, both about my mother and about my father, about the place we came from and that there were four of us children, that we were poor. I won't try to describe how things looked in Aana. You know, yourself, how difficult it is to describe a place. It's impossible even to describe a face so that someone else can actually recognize it. I tried to do that once with someone who was close to me. I could not do it; I had to consult her passport even to find out the color of her hair and her height."

He remained sitting in silence for a while, and his expression mirrored so clearly what he was thinking that he could have just as well said aloud, "I'm not sure whether or not I should say anymore." But then he continued: "We were talking about the place I came from: Aana. Yes, it had another name, but we simply called it Aana after the river that ran through the town. In the old days it was a center for smoked salmon and salted herring. In the days before plastic barrels. The great warehouses stood side-by-side from the mouth of the river out to the fjord, and straight on to the waterfall, a kilometer's walk up the road. Our house lay so close to the river that when there were floods, the water ran into our cellar. I can see that river in my mind's eye with absolute clarity, but strangely enough — always from one particular point, from the window in the narrow bedroom where we slept. I remember, too, that I heard the river run by at night with a kind of silken murmur, but that must have been my imagination, because the water flowed so slowly that one could barely see it move. Deep in the stream on the sandy bottom were heavy, round boulders that were covered with long, greenish ribbons of seaweed that were in constant motion, as if they were green fish swimming with the current. For that matter the stream was full of fish. Sometimes the trout swam all the way up on the bottom, right under our window. I remember one summer morning I woke suddenly and I was absolutely wide awake. It must have been about five o'clock, because the sun had just risen over the heath, on the 'winter side of the fjord,' as we used to say. Everyone in the house slept.

"I felt that now, that very moment, I had to look outside. The water was so clear that I could see every stick and pebble on the bottom, and I felt a remarkable sense of expectation. Suddenly, there in the dark, deep channel, out in the middle of the river, I spied the largest salmon I had ever seen. 'Now it's going to disappear,' I thought, but it didn't. It glided over the sandy bottom towards our house. It swam slowly over its own shadow on the pale river bottom, as if it wanted to display itself. I could distinguish every scale and every glint of color, the tremendous tail and the fins through which the sun glistened, and the scarlet flashes each time the gills opened. I crouched on my knees on my bed and I cried. With joy? With gratitude? I thanked God because he had awakened me so that I could see it.

"But it was not always like that. In the autumn when the river ran high and the wind blew against the land, the jelly fish came drifting in from the fjord. Floating side by side in the deep where there was salt water, they formed disgusting orange clusters, like plum jam. I often pressed my face against the window frame and watched them and wondered where they came from. Even when they weren't there, I thought about them.

"Down by the mouth of the river was the big warehouse that housed the cooperage where my father worked. They made barrels at the other warehouses as well, and when we rowed out on the river, we could hear the hollow noise as the workers hammered on the barrels and as they rolled them across the floor. An unusual echo rebounded from building to building on either side of the river. The warehouses were almost identical, with huge trap doors on the river side and thick ropes that hung from the extended gables as if they were gallows. When we boys wanted to prove ourselves, we would grab the loop in the rope and let ourselves be hoisted by our arms out of the boat and all the way up to the gable, where we swung and dangled until we were lowered again. Sometimes we sneaked up to the uppermost floor of a warehouse, and with the rope tight in our fists we took a running jump and swung through the open trapdoor. I still remember the mixture of terror and joy when I would arc out over the dark waters, and the sickening relief when I once more swung back through the trapdoor. Lars was a master at that. Once he let go and landed out in the middle of the stream. He risked his life. If he had fallen a few meters further, he would have crashed among the boulders, on the other side of the channel."

Once more he stopped, as if he regretted having spoken the name. He walked over to the night table and began to rummage through the drawer. He came up with a pipe and tobacco; earlier he had smoked only cigarettes. He filled the pipe slowly, lit it, but lay it aside with a grimace, and immediately lit a cigarette.

"Who was Lars?"

"Lars...?" He continued to smoke, stumped out the cigarette, and, once more, reached for the endless toothpicks.

"Lars was my brother."

He was two years older than I. He often did dangerous things like that. Perhaps that was one of the reasons he had such power over us; because he did have a remarkable power over people. Once we found some explosives, and he shoved half a stick of dynamite inside a barrel filled with sand. Then he put a top on the barrel and sat on it while he ordered one of the others to light the fuse. But no one wanted to do it, and finally he did it himself and then calmly climbed back on the barrel and waited while the fuse burned. I do not know how calm he really was. Perhaps he was afraid. We others, terrified, watched from a safe distance. I shouted for him to move away, but I knew it was useless, because he had that look that used to frighten me so, a kind of sleepy calm, as if he had difficulty holding his eyes open; his face grew red and there were pasty white spots on his cheeks.

Fortunately everything went well and he was tossed only a few centimeters up into the air. He was not particularly large. Nor was he the strongest. But, nevertheless, everyone was afraid of him and did as he said. He administered punishment if anyone broke the rules. Even if it was something that happened many days before, he never forgot. "There's something we have to take care of!" he would say, quietly, as if he were sorry about what was coming, but as if he were forced to perform a necessary chore. He lined us up and ordered the culprit forward. And then, after he announced what offense had been said or done, he struck him once or twice across the face with the flat of his hand. Sometimes he hit him three times on either cheek. I do not remember that anyone ever protested.

There were others we feared as well. Warehouse Arnt, for example. He owned the cooperage where my father worked. But our fear of him was of an entirely different nature. He never laid a hand on us, and we had no reason to be afraid, but, nevertheless, it was an unspoken law that we did not touch anything that belonged to him. We never dared to enter his warehouse after it was locked in the evening.

Old miser that he was, he had plenty of money but barely spent enough to feed himself. He lived in the warehouse, where he had partitioned off rooms and a kitchen in back of the shop. There were few who knew how it looked in there. No one visited him, and he had no associates. Evenings he perched on a sawed-off, quartered barrel that he positioned on the bare warehouse floor, just inside the opened trap door. We never saw him at the windows that faced towards town. He always sat in the same place and gazed out over the river and the fjord. He had unusual pale blue eyes, and they never teared the way other folk's did. I wondered how he could blink, and I often, secretly, watched his eyes when I was out at the cooperage with my father. "It doesn't pay," he used to say, and I wondered what he meant by that, because it was practically the only thing he ever said.

It certainly must have paid because his was the largest cooperage in town, and he always managed to buy his barrel staves at a cut rate. When the upland farmers came to him to sell, he could hardly be bothered with talking to them, "Go to someone else. I'm going to stop making barrels. It doesn't pay," he would say crossly and turn his back on them. He got the staves at the price he wanted. There was a surplus of staves, and the farmers depended on selling them.

It was the same when, rarely, one of his coopers complained about his wages. "Go to the others," he would say and turn his back. He paid forty øre a barrel while the others paid fifty. Afraid to complain, the coopers kept secret how much they earned because it was considered shameful to work for less than the others. If the truth were known, one would be looked down upon and considered an inferior cooper.

My father suffered more than the rest. It was as if he had never been trained. Whereas the other coopers finished seven barrels a day, he would make four or five. Often my mother nagged him to go to Arnt and ask for a raise. In the evenings, as I lay in bed next to Lars, we would hear these conversations. There was something in the relationship between Warehouse Arnt and my father that I did not understand. My father would lie, fully clothed, on the bed in the living room, and my mother would sit at the sewing machine.

"It's a shame that he pays you so little. You should go right up to him and tell him that!" my mother would say, and she would spin the wheel of the sewing machine with extra vigor.

Father seldom answered, but a few times he did respond. "*I* am supposed to talk to him? To *him?*"

"If there's anyone he should pay fairly, it's certainly you."

"Hush, they can hear you!"

"They're sleeping," my mother would reply angrily. "It wouldn't hurt if they did hear how he treats you. You! And Lars knows it."

It always ended the same way — father would talk his way out of it.

Did she believe all of his excuses — that his tools were not as good as the others', that the staves were full of knots and that the others managed to grab the hazel wood hoops that were easiest split?

"But all you think is that I'm a bad cooper. Shout it so they all can hear you. Why don't you open the window?"

It usually ended with mother in tears. "I certainly don't say that." We could hear how she struggled to muffle her sobs. "I know that if only you had the right tools you would do better! But you can never afford them. Everything you earn goes to us for food and clothing...."

"And then this headache — this heddek," as he would say, "this blasted heddek." Then he would cover his face with the newspaper. When mother was not spinning the machine, I could hear the rustle of the paper each time he exhaled. He would lie like that all evening, right up until the moment mother turned out the light and began to undress. But sometimes he would suddenly throw the paper aside and get up, as if there were some errand he had to attend to, something important that could not wait. Mother would always try to hold him back. "Don't go," she would cry. "I'll make some coffee. If you want, we can go right to bed." She was forever tempting him with coffee and sex.

He never listened to her, but he did take his own good time. Perhaps he enjoyed having her beg him to stay; possibly that was one of the few pleasures in his harassed and impoverished life. I used to watch him through the half-opened bedroom door, and I remember how he would stand in the middle of the room and pull on his knitted jacket and button his work smock, slowly, calmly, in order to prolong the moment.

Because we lay under the same blanket, I noticed how Lars always stiffened when father's wooden shoes retreated down the road beyond our house. Sometimes he dressed and ran out, even though he knew that father grew angry and threatened a beating whenever Lars sneaked out after him.

Lars always protected father. He became particularly irate whenever people made fun of father's dialect. Father had come to Aana when he was in his twenties and he never lost his native Lista pronunciation with its long drawn-out final "e" at the end of words. Anyone who imitated father's speech, even if only with the slightest of intonations in a single word, risked punishment if Lars heard about it.

Lars was also watchful when father was with other adults. Father was a different man when he was out among people; he never had a headache then. The men who stood outside the general store evenings with their hands stuck under their suspenders and folded on their stomachs became lively when father passed by. "Here comes Arnold," they smiled and winked at each other. "We were just talking about the mayor," they would say, although that had not been in their conversation. "What's your opinion, Arnold?" And immediately father would begin to hold forth, either about the mayor or about what was going on at church or at the meetings of the town commissioners. He would become particularly excited about the town commission. He was a phenomenal speaker. Sentences, well-phrased and fully formed, literally poured out of him. I often thought about that later when I sat and struggled with my sermons. When I approached the general store and heard the bursts of laughter, I knew that father was there. He stood in the middle of the throng, a handsome man with a tanned, full face, dark, curly hair, and perfect teeth which were particularly noticeable because he always smiled when he talked.

Lars stayed constantly near. He perched on the kerosene keg by the wall of the store, or else he sat, some distance away, astride his bicycle and on watch. Father often stayed for hours, even after the others had left. When we played in the schoolyard or, in autumn, spear-fished for trout in the river, I saw father there under the electric light. If Lars bicycled over and stopped nearby, father would chase him away, sometimes threatening him with a wooden shoe. Then Lars would cycle on, out to the church on the headland or to one of the cooperages on the far side of the river. When he returned, he stopped some distance away from the general store, outside the circle of light. He waited. He never left until father was on the way home.

Not until I was older did I understand some of the rumors that circulated about father and Warehouse Arnt. One day, as I was walking over to the cooperage to deliver lunch and a thermos for father, I passed the sawmill where a number of young men were piling up logs. "Are you going out to your grandfather's?" one of them shouted. "Who's that?" I asked, because I did not know that I had a grandfather. But all I got for an answer was mocking laughter, and I realized that there *was* someone. At the supper table silence fell when I reported the incident. My two sisters stopped eating and looked nervously at each other. "What kind of foolishness is that!" mother said sternly. No more was said. But later on, when we were in bed, Lars whispered that if I said anything about it again, I would get a beating: "three boxes on each ear." He always kept his word, but never exceeded his promise.

My father's mother came from Aana where there had been something between her and Arnt. When she was about twenty, she moved to Lista and worked there as a servant. She never returned to Aana. In the beginning, Arnt visited her. People still talked about how he would row all the way out there on Saturday nights. Someone was said to have come upon them in an isolated barn between Jøllestø and Rudjord. The visits stopped when she got pregnant. Arnt was not sure that it was his.

A while later she married the elderly widower in whose house she was the servant. I have checked in the church registry in Vanse, and he is listed there as my father's father. I never saw him; he died two years after father was born. I saw her only once. She was sick then, and it was decided that the entire family should visit her before she died.

It was a grand occasion, and we children were in such suspense that we could not sleep the night before our journey. My father was able to borrow a horse and cart from Jens Christian, the owner of the general store. The trip took all day. The weather was fine and we stopped twice. I still remember the places. At the first spot a band of Gypsies appeared and surrounded us. It was a deserted place by a stream with a small water wheel. The band of Gypsies was large, with three horses. My mother was frightened when she saw them coming. She whispered that father should not take out his wallet. Before we knew it, they swarmed over us. There were children and old people, and dark men with knives tucked under their belts. One of the old Gypsy women was terrible to see. Where her nose should have been there was nothing but two gaping holes. I saw her again in Aana many times. She was called "the noseless one." It was said that she had had cancer.

They were everywhere. They begged; they wanted to buy and sell — horse blinders and whips, copper pots; they touched our clothing and the harness on the horse and finally they tried to barter with father over a watch. When father was not interested, they grew angry and began to threaten. I remember, as well, that our horse and one of theirs bit each other and rose on their hind legs neighing. In order to appease the Gypsies, we gave them the rest of our food and a bag of coffee that we had brought along for grandmother.

Late in the afternoon we reached the flatland. I sat with my legs dangling through the boards of the cart, and I listened to the squeaking of the wheels and to the wind and the low booming from the waves down by the beach. I could not believe my eyes — that anything could be like that, so vast and powerful. Gulls, gliding sideways over the stone fences and the broad fields of heather, flew over as if they were curious about us. Then they careened up into the wind again, out towards the beach and the green and white waves, where the sun broke gleaming over the pebbles, lighting them with a blinding flash.

The house of my father's mother stood apart, some distance from the shore. A small birch stood outside the kitchen window, bent by the winds and gnarled into tight knots, like minute birds' nests. I thought the tree resembled grandmother, because she also was crooked and walked bent to one side. She was frightfully thin, but with large hands and feet. Sometimes she pressed her bony fists against her ribs and rested motionless, while she gazed through eyes that were narrow slits.

Mother scolded her when we arrived because we did not find her in her bed. "Was that why you came, to talk to me like that?" grandmother retorted. She was angry. She did not need us, and we could turn right around and go back home. "If you intend to stay, then act like decent folk."

During the days we were there, everyone talked in whispers. Only when she was out of the house did my mother and father dare to speak aloud, but even then their voices were muted. "Look at her," father said, incensed. He stood by the kitchen window. She and Lars were down on the beach harvesting kelp. "What is she going to do with the kelp? She's not going to have any use for it!"

Grandmother sat on a rock while Lars loaded the wheelbarrow. They had fastened a rope to the front, and when they returned with a load, she pulled, doubled over with the rope on her shoulder, while Lars steered. The wheelbarrow was constantly tipping so that they had to load up again, and sometimes she fell over and Lars had to help her back up on her feet. Mother wanted father to intervene, but father refused: "What good would it do? Let her do it. Just let her keep it up. Then we'll see how long they last," he announced triumphantly. Hours he waited for her to be unable to rise. "I'll have to throw out a rope and drag her back. I certainly can't carry her."

But each time she got up again, struggling and crawling while Lars pulled. He stuck with her like a shadow. In the evening they stayed in the courtyard between the barn and the house. The yard was enclosed by a plank fence on each side. A smell of burning turf came from the open hearth where she cooked potatoes for the pigs. She was always busy with something, tidying up, rattling around with a bucket, shifting hay with a pitchfork or a rake. "Does it hurt?" Lars asked each time she hunched up and pressed her hands into her side. "It's better when it hurts; then you know where you're at."

Once I was out by the barn though they did not know it, and I heard grandmother and Lars talking in the yard. They each sat on a herring box in front of the open fire. She asked him about people in Aana, mentioning name after name. When Lars would say that someone was dead, she merely grunted a short, "So... yes, yes."

"And Arnt?"

"Warehouse Arnt?"

"That's what they call him. He keeps to himself?"

"Father works for him as a cooper."

"And they talk together? Perhaps you've heard what they say?"

"They never talk."

"So, then, he makes barrels for Arnt?" When Lars did not reply, she said sharply, "Is he any good at making barrels, your father?"

"No," Lars answered sorrowfully. "I help him split the barrel hoops," he said after a while. "That, especially, he can't manage."

They were quiet for so long that I thought they had gone inside. But then she began to cough from the peat smoke, and when the attack was finally over I heard her voice again. "You should stay here with me. Then we could harvest kelp."

"I can come to you again when we have off from school during the potato harvest."

"That's no good. I won't be here."

"Where are you going?"

"Down into the earth." She began to cough again.

When our family returned to Aana, she pretended not to see us leave. Only after the horse had begun to move did she come out to the gate in the yard. She stood and watched us until we were so far away that she seemed to blend into the planking of the fence.

Lars sat furthest back in the cart, turned away from the direction we were traveling. He cried noiselessly, with an immobile face. I thought about what she said — that she would be going down into the earth, and that Lars, too, would someday have earth covering his eyes. It was the first time I saw him cry.

Grandmother died shortly after that, and father traveled alone to the funeral. He returned with a sofa and some chairs. That was all he got. Grandmother's husband, the widower, had arranged that everything would go to the children of his first marriage. So, he, too, probably doubted that father was his son.

Why did Lars treat me the way he did? What had I done to him? Had I done something to him that I did not realize? I often wondered about that, and I still think about it today. But I still do not understand. Why did he treat me differently than he did my two sisters? He was kind to them, made things for them and helped them with their arithmetic.

The girls slept together in one bed on the other side of the room. Before they slept they scratched each other's backs. "Scratch me," Ingrid, the oldest, would whisper. "No, not there, higher up, there, right under the shoulder blade!" Afterwards it was Ida's turn. They lay like that and whispered and giggled.

There was always distance between Lars and me, but I could still feel the warmth from his body. He seemed as hot as an oven. Often I would have liked to turn to him, to talk with him. Only once did I try. It was an autumn evening. The flooded river roared by, and I placed my hand on his arm and whispered, "Listen," but he pretended he was asleep. I was sure he was awake. I always knew. I knew when he stared at me, as well. I could feel his gaze as surely as I could the heat from his body.

Once father had to work all night. We went to the cooperage to help out. There was a shipment going out the next day, and it was necessary to finish as many barrels as possible. The cutter was tied up outside the warehouse, and my job was to help with the loading. It was fun to roll the barrels across the warehouse floor and send them down the ramp to the hold where two men stacked them, higher and higher, until the shipment lay even with the top floor of the warehouse. In the shop room they all worked against time, and Lars helped father band the barrels. As capable as any of the adult coopers, Lars split the hazel wood stakes right down the middle and flattened them with his knife.

Father talked the entire time, about everything and nothing, about the number of barrels they had sent in the last shipment, and how many they had sent at one time or another in the past year. The others worked in silence, and I realized that his talking irritated them. They glanced at each other.

Without a word, Arnt, poking around in his wooden shoes, shuffled from bench to bench with a coffee cup in hand. Abruptly he stopped next to father. "If you were as good with your hands as you are with your mouth, you would be a decent cooper!" He spoke loud enough for everyone to hear. The room became silent – only the tread of Arnt's wooden shoes. The two men from the cutter, who had come up to eat, stopped and glanced furtively to right and left. They understood that something was up. One of the coopers smiled, and another began to hum.

Father turned white. He smiled and acted as if nothing were wrong, but he kept quiet. Everyone knew that Arnt's reprimand would be talked about for a long time to come. Arnt continued to shuffle about with his coffee cup, and when he passed the pile of waste slivers where I was sitting, he stopped. "It's so quiet over here. You should liven things up, Eilif. How does that verse go?"

I pretended that I did not hear, but he refused to give up. "The verse about Liste and the twigs...!" It was a rhyme the youngsters recited mimicking the Lista dialect:

> At Liste-e
> They have no twiggies
> There they whip the brats raw
> With a handful of peat sod,
> So that they will shiver-e with fright-e.

He kept watching me, and I recited the verse softly and quickly so that Lars would not hear. He was sitting in the far corner, beside father.

One of the coopers laughed so hard that he almost choked on his meal and Arnt said to me, "You're a fine whip of a lad. Since you're so clever at reciting verses, I'll have to find a present for you."

Father laughed, too, but he had changed. He no longer talked. The others, noticing his silence, called across the room, asking him about one thing or another. Father answered in monosyllables. He had become the way he was at home when he lay in bed and stared at the ceiling.

I continued to roll barrels, but I worried about what I had done. I had mocked father.

On my way home I noticed that someone was bicycling behind me, and I started running when I saw it was Lars. But I stopped, both because I knew it was no use to run away and because I wanted to get it over with. He would give me at least three blows on each ear, and I decided that would be reasonable. He stopped next to me, and I waited. But nothing happened.

When I looked into his face, I saw no anger, and I was absolutely dumbfounded when he asked me to jump up behind him on the bicycle. I could not remember the last time that had happened. He did not even object when I held on to his hips to balance myself. He just whistled.

Instead of turning down the side street to our house, he continued on in the direction of the waterfall.

"Where are we going?"

"Up to Tverrdalen. There's something I want to show you."

I was astonished that he would talk to me as if we were friends, as if we shared a secret. I also thought it strange that he knew about Tverrdalen. It was a ravine that entered the river just above the waterfall. It was my secret place, and I did not know that he went there, too. Up there I always felt safe — I could talk to myself and listen to my own voice. But even if no one else could hear me — the falls below drowned out everything — I always spoke softly, because what was spoken in that place was so special. I had a chosen spot right under the cliff, where the brook ran into a deep pool, and when I had something good to eat — a Danish pastry or a white roll, I would break off a few pieces and throw them out in the pool. One for mother, for father, for my sisters, for Lars — I always named Lars last. I ate the rest. That was my portion. I also had a pocket knife and other small things hidden under a flat stone that I had covered with moss. Was that what Lars had found? Did he intend that we would share the spot from now on?

Strewn with enormous rocks, the slope was almost impassable, but Lars climbed ahead, more quickly than I could follow. I noticed that he knew precisely the right footholds. Had he been here often? Perhaps he had spied on me, listened when I sat and talked to myself? He climbed so fast that I had to shout and plead that he wait. Then he stopped and poked in the rocks with his stick. It was a hazel wood stick that he had taken from the warehouse. It had been soaking, and it was very flexible.

Dusk came and I shouted that we had to turn back, even though I knew that once he had decided that we would climb up there, there was no use in complaining. I remembered what I had done down at the warehouse, and I began to be frightened. All the time he was ahead of me. Only when we had reached the cliff did he stop and wait, and then, when I came closer and saw his face, I turned and ran. But it was too late. He took my arm and held it tight. "Recite the verse!" he said calmly. I could not say one word, but he insisted, and so I obeyed him. He lay into me with the stick as soon as I had finished. The blow hit me on the outside of my hand. It hurt so much that I ran. But I stumbled and fell down. Immediately I felt an excruciating sting across my backside. I screamed, but I knew it was no use; no one could hear us; the waterfall drowned out everything. When I tried to crawl off, he beat me across my legs and so I lay flat, and then he rained blows down over me, over my back and sides and my behind. Each time I screamed, he hit me. I could not stop even though I knew that each scream meant a fresh blow. "Take that, and that...!" he cried. Then, finally, he stopped.

He sat on a rock next to the brook and poked in the moss with the stick. Then he threw it out into the pool. It sank slowly through the clear water and lay on the bottom. "Why did you do that?" I sobbed. He whistled softly. Then he stood up and walked off, and I pulled myself to my feet and hurried after him, afraid that he would leave me. I thought that I might tell mother, but perhaps he guessed what I was thinking, because just then he turned and looked at me, and immediately I swore that I would not tell. He put his foot up on a rock, and I thought that he was going to tie his shoe, but instead he pulled the lace out. Was he going to tie me up and leave me there? I shouted again and again that I would not tell. But he let the shoelace dangle in front of my face.

"Don't do it!" I turned away, but he ordered me to look at him.

"Don't do it'"

"Not now. But at night. I'll tie you up and throw you in the river. And you'll drift out to sea." Even though I knew that he would not do that, I was terrified.

"I won't tell."

"Do you promise?"

"I promise!"

Afterwards he helped me wash my face in the stream so that no one would know that I had cried. In the evening, when mother noticed that it hurt me to sit, she asked me what was the matter, and I said that I had fallen from my bicycle. When it was time for us to go to bed, Lars lifted up his pillow. There lay the shoelace.

The pain kept me up late into the night, but, none-theless, I felt a remarkable sense of security. I was not afraid — not of the shoelace under the pillow, not of Lars. He lay with his back to me and slept. I knew that God would take care of me, and that nothing truly bad or dangerous could happen to me. I prayed fervently. That was, indeed, the first time I truly prayed.

After that day, things were different between Lars and me. He never hit me again. He avoided me, and did not want me to look at him. I noticed that from the way he turned in bed, quickly and with some force, as people do in sleep. But I knew that he only pretended to sleep. I tested it many times in the dark. Whenever I stared at him for a while, he turned around, always in the same way.

I no longer let myself be bothered by what he said, or, in any case, not as before. Perhaps that was because, at about that time, I became friends with Didrik.

I knew very well who Didrik was. The whole countryside knew him. He was an old man who lived on a farm called Hausebakken, a mile and a half from Aana. Every Sunday morning he walked down the steep slope. He was so dependable that people set their clocks by him; when he appeared it was exactly one hour before church began. His wife and small daughter had died of the Spanish influenza a year after his marriage. He was at sea when it happened and came home a month after the funeral. After that he abandoned the sea, and when a new organ was installed in the church, he got a job ringing the bells and pumping the bellows; it was said that he chose to work as sexton so that he could be near his loved ones in the church graveyard.

Before the service, Didrik always visited the graves. There he sat on a rock and smoked his pipe. Some people complained because he smoked in the grave-yard, and others gossiped because he had not bought a gravestone. Neither did he plant flowers. But he did keep the graves clean and free of weeds. People were not really angry with him. He was loved and respected by everyone.

I had seen Hausebakken, but I had never been there. A portion of the barn roof was visible from the main road. But I did not know that one could go there through Tverrdalen. A long time had passed since I had been to Tverrdalen. I did not want to go there again. The place was no longer mine. But then, after a while, I began to wonder if what had happened with Lars was real. Was it only something I had imagined?

Early one Sunday morning, before anyone was awake, I walked up to Tverrdalen. It was the end of April. The birches were not yet green, but the anemone was in bloom. It was mild, almost like summer, with clear skies and the song of birds. The day before it had rained and there was a rumbling and foaming down among the rocks where the stream was not visible. When I reached the pool, I saw the stick right away. The green hazel bark glistened in the sunshine. Quickly, I removed my shoes and waded out and threw the stick up over the embankment, but it rolled down again and lay, bobbing, on a shelf of rock. I wanted to climb up and throw it further out, but just then I heard a faint bleating above me. I was not sure I heard properly, but when I climbed up along the edge of the stream with my shoes in my hand, I heard it more clearly. A little farther on I saw the sheep. On the ground, beside it, lay a lamb. Bluebottle flies hummed and shimmered in the air around it. It must have been newborn because it was wet and could not stand. It struggled to get to its feet, but tumbled over on its side.

I lifted it carefully, but the ewe began to bleat. The lamb struggled, and I felt the heart beating wildly in the wet, warm body. The mother cried pitifully, but quieted when I began to climb out of the ravine. She jumped ahead, bleated again, and turned. But she ran further when she saw that I followed. I had no idea where the ravine was leading. Neither did I wonder about it. I just followed the stream. At some places it was so narrow between the sides of the mountain and the stream that I had to wade, and my feet were numb from the cold water. It was shady here and violet anemones thickly covered the banks and the cliffs. Here and there, small, pointed blades of lily of the valley pushed up through the rotted leaves.

The lamb was almost dry now, but it was heavy to carry, and I was drenched with sweat. I could not help but stumble, and I scraped my knees and they stung. The lamb seemed at peace. It fluttered its ears to chase away the flies — it knew how to do that already. The eye that faced me was clear and shone with delicate colors, like the sand on the bottom of the pool. When I lay down to rest, the ewe came over and sniffed the lamb, and it turned to nurse, and when I started climbing again there were tiny drops of milk in the hairs around its mouth.

It was still early morning. Everything was clear and distinct against the sharp shadows. It seemed I had walked for an endlessly long time, but it could not have been more than an hour. The narrow valley opened up and I reached a cultivated field, and just after that I saw a man emerge from the thicket. It was Didrik. He had heard the bleating and realized that something was amiss. "You can always hear by the bleating when a ewe gives birth to a lamb," he said.

He told me to come home with him, that he would find a slice of bread for me. It was only a short distance to Hausebakken. The house was small and painted white with green trim. The yard was freshly raked, farm tools and containers hung on the unpainted wall of the barn and the firewood was neatly stacked over by the shed. I thought how messy it was outside our house — we never seemed able to tidy up the disorder. The stream that I had followed ran below the house. So, this is where it comes from, I thought, and I decided that it was appropriate that it should originate precisely here. A stone bridge crossed the stream, and just below lay a hollow, wooden chute from which the water ran down into a pool in which a tub was placed for cooling milk.

Immediately the ewe began to drink from the pool. It was as if she had waited to quench her thirst until she arrived safely home. I was thirsty, too, but I could not kneel down with my scraped knees, and so I bent under the chute and let the water stream into my mouth. Didrik shouted that I should stop because it was dangerous for someone sweating to drink too much cold water.

I sat down next to Didrik on the steps while he held the lamb and checked to see whether it was a ewe or a ram. His hands were a little crooked, and he chuckled when the lamb began to suck on his finger. Then he went inside to make me some butter-bread.

His parlor was filled with strange and wonderful things that he had gotten during the years he had gone to sea. Photographs of the ships he had served on hung on the walls. There was also a wedding picture of him and his wife. I was looking at it when he came in with the slices of bread and a glass of milk.

"We never had a chance to take any pictures of Lydia." That was one of the few times he mentioned his family in all the years I knew him.

When I had first seen him in the field he asked who I was. Now he asked again. "So then, you're the son of Henriette and Arnold? I remember when you were christened."

I had also heard something about that. Mother had once mentioned it to a neighbor woman. It had been so mysterious in the church, she had said. God's spirit had been so noticeably present that everyone had felt it.

Now I tried to question Didrik, but he did not want to talk about it.

"You come to church with me and pump the bellows," was all he said. Then he walked down to the chute and washed himself.

That was how I met Didrik. It was in my third year of school. I was born at the end of May, so it must have been just before I turned ten.

I visited him often. Even in the fall and winter I was there at least once a week. It is, perhaps, those autumn trips I remember best — when the stream in Tverrdalen was frozen, and icicles, yellow with drippings from the moss, hung down from the steep cliffs. Hoarfrost never melted there where the sun did not penetrate during the entire winter half of the year.

When I stood on the bridge and looked out over the yard and heard that Didrik was home — and he was always there when I came — I thought how fortunate I was, how unimaginably fortunate. Later, when I grew older and understood better, I realized that perhaps my pleasure had something to do with father, that Didrik gave me a feeling of security that I had long missed. But I did not think about that then.

We always had something to do, and when we were finished outside I went in with him for lunch. What did we talk about? I no longer remember. I did most of the talking. "In a half hour I have to light the lamp," he would always say, and that meant that now I had to leave in order to reach home before dark. On Sundays, when I saw him up at Kleiva, by the church, I waited a while because I knew he wanted to be alone in the graveyard. But he always unlocked the church door so that I could go inside. Thus, I was alone in the church before he came. I would stand in the center aisle, just inside the door, and gaze up at the choir and baptismal font, and I was filled with solemn pride when I thought about what mother had said. There it had happened. God had been present on that special occasion and had filled the church with His mighty spirit. I never dared go up there. But in the rear gallery, I felt safe. That was our place.

We had a small room behind the organ, right under the church steeple. It was dark and cramped. High in the tower was a vent that threw a pale light in over the two bells that were barely visible among the great beams. A ladder led up to a platform where the bell ropes dangled. The bells were heavy and it took a while to get them swinging properly. I marveled that the sound could be heard so far away because, inside, it was not so loud. But yet, I recognized the power within them; when I propped my hand against the thick wooden beams, I felt how they quivered, and even the platform on which we stood vibrated slightly.

I liked best to pump the bellows. There was a balance beam that rested over a bench, almost like a swing. At first I could not pump it alone. I stood behind the beam and clung to Didrik. We rose and fell with the bellows. It was as if a great animal were breathing. When I was older I was permitted to do it alone. When I saw how the bellows rose and the sound of the organ filled the church, I felt such happiness that tears often filled my eyes.

One autumn night Warehouse Arnt disappeared. The coopers came to the shop towards seven in the morning and he was not there. The trapdoor facing the river was open and his wooden shoes stood in the middle of the floor, as if he had just stepped out of them.

When they had said good-night to him the evening before, no one noticed anything unusual. Nevertheless, he had been more taciturn recently. He no longer left the warehouse. When he had to shop, he sent one of the youngsters to the general store with a list. He also talked continuously about how he would stop making barrels; it was no longer profitable. But no one paid much attention to him, because barrel prices were high and he had repeated the same thought so many times before.

It had rained during the night, and the river had begun to rise. The rainy weather continued during the morning, and heavy clouds clung to the hills and mountains on the far side of the fjord. When Lars and I arrived at the warehouse in the gray morning light, people had gathered on the wharf to lend a hand. It was so quiet — no knocking and pounding from the other shops. Everyone took part in the search. Coils of rope and grappling hooks were loaded into the boats and if someone spoke it only concerned the job at hand and how the equipment should be rigged.

Father watched the preparations, but he did not participate. It was as if the search did not concern him. Someone told him to jump on board. The man held the boat still against the current and shouted that he had to hurry, but father did not answer, and then the man lost his grip on the wharf and the boat careened sideways down the river until they got it on an even keel. Lars wanted father to come with him in another boat, but he turned and walked down the alley towards home.

At least ten boats were assembled outside the mouth of the river. The sheriff led the search. He stood up in the boat wearing his sheriff's cap and oilskins, his knees supported against the thwarts so that he would not fall overboard. With his loud and powerful voice he shouted and directed the boats into place. They formed a half-circle in mid-current at the mouth of the river. The boats lay so tight that they hardly had room to dip their oars in the water. On order, the grappling hooks sank into the sea, and then they began to row into the river and towards the warehouse. It was hard work because the current was swift, the river climbed every hour and the dredging held them back. Some boats fell behind when they hooked something, and when they stopped, the current drove them downstream again. But they found only scrap, tangled nets and other debris that had been thrown in during the course of time. They searched from land as well. Men took boat hooks and rowed among the warehouses and in the shallows. But it was difficult to see anything, because the day was dark and the bay was covered with spray and drizzle.

Towards noon it stopped raining, but the low and lingering cloud-cover threw a bleak half-light over the fjord. Nevertheless the mood gradually lightened. The men shouted to each other from the boats, and from a few houses came calls to come in for dinner. There was laughter when a boat reached one of the wharves where the womenfolk, shivering in their sweaters, stood waiting with hot coffee. Then, little by little, they gave up. They had done their best. No one could reproach them if they did not continue any longer – they knew very well that he must have drifted out to sea.

That was the first time I experienced death and understood that there was another reality behind all that was safe and ordinary. There had always, to be sure, been deaths, but they were unexceptional. They were part of everyday existence. When someone died we had time off from school because the teacher was the singer in church and took part in the funeral service.

I was often with Didrik and rang the bells. I would stand watch to report when the funeral procession approached so that he could begin to ring the bells, and I would feel no uneasiness. I knew, as if it were fact, that the dead would at some time rise, and, rejoicing to meet again, they would stream out into the graveyard. I often thought about that, and it always filled me with excitement. It never dawned on me that I, myself, would be there. Didrik and I would be in the tower, ringing the bells while those down below swarmed forth. And afterwards Didrik, slowly and with solemnity, would climb down the stairs and walk over to the graves to meet his wife and daughter while I stayed behind and pumped the organ bellows. Everything was exultation and celebration.

Did I really believe that? Or did I, even then, realize that it was only illusion, fantasy? I am not sure. But I do know that what I felt after Arnt departed became reality. After his disappearance, death became silence and darkness, and it filled me with horror. I often thought about how it must have been the night he did it, and it was always the same in my imagination: silence and darkness. He sat there in his room behind the cooperage with a coffee cup in his hand and stared, dry-eyed, into space. Through the window he could see the electric light at the general store where father often was. Then he stood up and walked out to the shop. He did not stumble. He knew the way. Why did he take off his wooden shoes? Why did he step out of them in the middle of the floor? Was he afraid of the sound of his own footsteps? Did he think that the shoes might float up to the surface and be found? He approached the trapdoor, pushed it up, it squeaked on its pulley, and he opened it half way. Then he did it. And just as he fell, he grabbed the hoisting rope that hung down from the apex of the gable. But it jerked out of his hand and it swung forward and back. When it was once more hanging motionless, he was already out in the stream and everything was as before — the warehouse, the lamp in front of the general store, the piles of barrel staves.

Everything appears before me noiseless and colorless. His eyes, alone, gleam in their blueness. I see the amorphous body that moves in the current down on the bottom of the fjord, the arms and the legs with their gray woolen socks move sluggishly, slowly, like jelly fish. Then the body drifts further in the current, outwards, steadily outwards to the darker deep, past Varnes and Elleholmene, outwards towards the land's end of Lista. Still something cries out in me in protest against The Almighty who has breathed His spirit into us so that we can see ourselves, see ourselves as we are. That *this* should be what we see! That such a thing can happen!

Things were more difficult for us after Warehouse Arnt was gone. When we returned home that evening, father lay gazing at the ceiling, and I saw that mother had been crying. She realized, already, how things were going to be. She knew that now our troubles would begin.

Father went to work as usual the next morning, but he returned home right away. The sheriff had sealed the door to the warehouse. For the time being there would be no barrel making. The sheriff thought that perhaps others would take over the cooperage, but that was not at all certain. He advised the men to find work elsewhere. And so they did. One emigrated to America, one went to sea, and three found work as barrel makers with other master coopers.

In the beginning, mother nagged father to find work before all the jobs were taken. Everyone knew, she assured him, how capable he was. But he no longer tried. He lay in bed most of the time, often until it was evening. Then he dressed and strolled over to the general store where he waited, alone, under the lamp in the dark autumn night. As time went by that happened less frequently, and finally he no longer went out at all.

Mother took in sewing. I always heard the hum of the sewing machine. Often she worked late into the night when an order had to be filled. They no longer quarreled, and neither did she pester him to find a job. Later there was less sewing, because another seamstress, one with training, had come to town — there was less and less fabric and material on the table at home.

During the school vacation, Lars and I worked for Jens Christian, the shopkeeper. He was the most important man in the district: treasurer of the township, director of the fund for the poor, bank manager. He also was actively engaged in truck farming. In those days people often left for America, and he leased or bought their farms. In the summer he employed as many as ten or twelve people, mostly women and children who worked for a few øre an hour.

By the end of the summer, mother also worked for him, but she had arthritis in her knee, and it was difficult for her to plant and weed. She crouched in the field, supporting herself with her left hand, while the stiff leg struggled along behind. She often complained that she was tired.

But she managed to remain cheerful, and what pleased her most was Lars. Whenever neighbors dropped by, she boasted how helpful and capable he had become and how satisfied Jens Christian was with him.

A remarkable transformation took place in Lars after father fell ill and little by little slid into apathy and darkness. Lars rarely went out, and he was never together with the rest of us, except when we were working at Jens Christian's. But even there, he kept to himself. He never concocted crazy schemes as he had so often done in the past.

At the same time, he did things that frightened me, and that I could not, at the time, understand because they seemed senseless. I remember one summer when we were working together at Jens Christian's. We were angry with Jens Christian because he always spied on us. We would take a break and he would always turn up without warning. "So the foxes of the sun have carried you all off like a silly flock of chickens!" he would laugh scornfully. We never felt safe from him, and we often plotted revenge. For the most part we talked about how, when we were grown up, we would give him a good thrashing. We evaded him as much as possible and we set out a watch. Lars never participated. He worked while we sunned ourselves. Jens Christian boasted about him. But I noticed the glance Lars sent after him when his back was turned.

In the spring we planted cabbage on a warm, sunny hillside at the base of a mountain slope. There was also a patch of cabbage below on the plain, but that was infected with club root. It was a sad sight. Everywhere were withered cabbage plants, and when we pulled them up, the roots were rotten clumps. Jens Christian told Lars to burn them so that the disease would not spread, and Lars built a bonfire while I pulled up the plants and carried them over to him.

I could not understand why he tore off the rotten clumps of root and only threw the tops of the plants in the fire. "Why are you doing that?" I asked, thinking that that must be the way it should be done.

"Don't you worry yourself about that," was all he answered.

In the dusk of evening, as I was walking home from Hausebakken, I caught sight of Lars on his way up to the hillside cabbage patch. He had a bucket in his hand. I ran after him, thinking that he was going up to the woods to pick berries. Then I came closer, and I saw him at the top of the cabbage patch; he went from row to row, dug a hole and slipped something into it. He was startled when I approached, but continued when he saw it was me. "You'd better shut up about this! You know what will happen if you tell!" he mumbled.

During the night it rained, and the next evening, in the twilight, I went to the field to dig up the diseased roots. I threw them down a rocky slope. Lars sneered at me when I came in late at night. I think he knew where I had been, but he never said anything.

Later I often worked up by the cabbage patch. The lush plants bristled and glistened, especially in the rain when the rows had been freshly hoed. But once, later in the summer, when we were weeding carrots nearby, I noticed a withered yellow cabbage plant in the midst of all the green. Without any of the others noticing, I walked over and pulled it up.

Later there were more. Dry midsummer came. And then the field withered.

Lars hated Jens Christian, then, when he worked for him, and later when he grew up, as well. It was a hatred he could never be rid of, and for which there was really no cause. Because Jens Christian was always nice to him.

Perhaps it was because Jens Christian was director of the fund for the poor, and it was to him that mother had to turn when we needed help. Mother never admitted that we received public assistance though everyone knew it. I remember the first time she asked for help. It was the Saturday before Palm Sunday and we had nothing in the house except some oatmeal. She took her shopping basket and walked over to Jens Christian's general store to find out if "he could use her for spring planting." She was pale and frightened when she set out, and she paused in the doorway and returned to sit down at the kitchen table for a while. Finally she left, and when she returned she was red-faced and distraught. "He gave me an advance," she said, while she unpacked the basket and lined up the groceries in the pantry.

She always received an advance, even when she could no longer work. Most often she went herself, but occasionally she would send one of us children with a

note. We understood what was going on. I felt it as soon
as I entered the general store and delivered the note to
Jens Christian. "So, you want another advance," he
would say with a smile, and those who stood around also
smiled. We noticed it at school, too. We received our
school supplies from the teacher instead of buying them
as the others did. When we wanted a new pencil or a
note book, we had to go up to the teacher's desk and
ask for it. It was worse for Lars. He always sneered
scornfully when the teacher carefully leafed through the
old book to see if he had used it properly. The teacher
would flush with anger because Lars sneered, but he
never dared strike him. "You know who's paying for
this," the teacher would say, and if there was one single
page in the book that was not filled with writing, he held
it up so the class could see it.

We were pitifully poor, but we never experienced
real need. We did not go hungry. When I visited Didrik,
he often gave me something to bring home — potatoes,
milk, a piece of butter. At Christmas he gave us a quarter
lamb. I was not ashamed to take it.

Didrik always asked about father and how things
were with his headaches. He was, in fact, the only one
who believed they existed. Most thought father's headaches were nothing but an excuse, that he was lazy and
did not want to work. When I talked about father, Didrik
often said: "Yes, yes, life is good only so long as things
go well." The words were simple. They could have been
said by anyone, but even today, forty-five years later,
people in Aana repeat his expression whenever some-

one suffers hardship or is struck down by calamity. "I agree with old Didrik that life is good only so long as things go well," they say.

And life was good. When I think about it, I realize I never felt unfortunate or humiliated. I recall my childhood as a happy time despite the misfortune that struck us.

Something happened in church one Whitsunday. As usual on similar festivals, it was crowded. Only the two highest pews, under the pulpit, were empty.

The minister was in the vestry changing, and there was a pause before he went up to the pulpit. The hymn had been sung, and, as usual, I sat next to Didrik on the back bench, up in the loft by the organ. I sensed a noticeable restlessness in the church. People whispered, turning around in the pews and staring at something, but I was so far back that I could not see what it was. The minister stared in the same direction as he walked towards the pulpit. But he was calm. As usual he nodded and smiled slightly to Elna, his daughter, with whom I attended school, and who later would become my wife. Then he entered the pulpit and began to pray.

He was not old, but he seemed old — and dignified, the way most prefer a minister to be. He had a deep, pleasant voice, and gray hair that he brushed back from his high forehead. He moved in a way that seemed absent-minded. Sometimes he knelt so long in front of the altar that people grew restless. He also had a habit of closing his eyes when he spoke so that it was difficult to know whether he was praying or preaching.

Now he spoke of the miracle of Pentecost, and he took as his text the passage in the hymn, "As the golden sun breaks forth." He proceeded to recite several verses even though we had just sung them. He repeated them slowly, as if he experienced within himself the sun which broke forth and put the darkness to flight. In fact, he rarely spoke of anything but of light and darkness. The darkness was the enemy of life. It was death, itself, and evil. And the sun and the light were proof of God's love. His sermons were short and people were often disappointed, especially those who had come a great distance. This time he was especially brief, and he was about to give the blessing when I heard father's voice from below in the church.

At first I thought I heard wrong, but when I moved forward I saw my father, and in the same instant I realized that he had gone mad. Recently, he had been restless and had begun to go outside again.

Now, he stood in the empty pew, directly in front of the mayor. It was as if he addressed him. He spoke with a loud, forceful voice, straining himself so that everyone would understand what he said. His face was darkly tanned and sweat glistened on his forehead. He appeared to smile as he spoke, but I knew that his expression was illusory. Although what he said was nonsense, I recall his words. He was pleased with the minister's sermon, he began. Certainly both the mayor and the entire congregation would agree with him when he thanked the minister for his fine words. But there was something in the sermon that ought to be clarified, something that, so far as he knew, was never discussed in the town council. "Isn't that right?" he said and turned to the mayor, who shifted restlessly and stared at the floor. Could it be that the minister was mistaken, father continued. Because it was becoming increasingly clear that what was said was often the direct opposite of what was correct! He used the word "correct" many times. Was it correct to say that the sun was light, when sunshine was known to be dark? Answer that? That was something everyone surely knew. Even scientists were clear about that. Why hide the truth when, sooner or later, it would come out?

It was uncannily quiet in the church while he spoke, but little by little the congregation grew restless. People whispered, some half rose and then sank back in their seats and watched the minister who stood motionless in the pulpit. In the beginning the minister looked as if he might interrupt father, but then he merely stood there. The teacher got up from his place as choir director and came forward. Presumably he planned to throw father out, but the minister raised his hand, and, red in the face, the teacher stopped and indignantly watched as the minister kept his hand raised to prevent his advance.

"What does our pastor know about light and darkness?" father cried in a loud voice. He began to talk about the town council again and about a road that should be built. "But of what use is it to build a road? Where does the road lead to?" he shouted. A woman began to cry, and he turned slowly towards her. "I see that Nikola weeps. We should all weep!" he said and began to recite the Our Father. The sweat poured down his face and he barely managed to pronounce the words. In the middle of the prayer, he stopped and looked around, as if, for the first time, he realized where he was and what he was doing. Then, defeated, he slowly walked down the middle aisle with bowed head. The minister still held up his arm. When father had gone out the door, the minister raised his other arm and pronounced the benediction.

After the church service, Didrik went down and spoke with the minister. The mayor and Jens Christian were there as well. The teacher, too, insisted on joining the conversation, and the others had to silence him; he responded sharply but then he left them and began to fuss with the hymnals over by the cupboard. It reminded me of how he behaved at his desk in the classroom when he was angry.

I was supposed to return with Didrik to Hausebakken, but he thought it would be best if I went home. Perhaps mother needed me. The atmosphere in our house was dismal, and the radiant summer weather outside only made things worse. A neighbor woman who had been in the church sat at the kitchen table opposite mother who, sobbing, buried her face on her arm. The woman held mother's hand. My sisters walked on tiptoe and whispered together; they began to remove the plates from the table in the living room where father lay trembling on the bed. His eyes were closed and he moaned. Lars, too, was lying down. I saw him, on the bed in our room, his face to the wall.

I could not bear staying there any longer, and I ran outside, up through Tverrdalen to Hausebakken. Didrik had not yet arrived, and I sat on the doorstep and waited. The swallows circled over the farmyard, joyful, as if nothing had happened, and the flowing water murmured in the pool. I thought about father's words about light and sunshine, and suddenly I realized he had been right. The sunshine, in fact, was dark.

Things got better when Didrik finally came. He was serious, but he did not talk about what had happened; while dinner cooked we took a walk out to the fields and looked after the sheep. In the afternoon he put on his best clothes again, and without saying anything, we began to walk, over the bridge and up the cart path, to the main road.

"Where are we going?" I asked, but I understood that we were going home.

"I want to talk with him. And with your mother. I believe it is best for everyone if he leaves."

"Will he go to the asylum?" The word filled me with horror.

"That would be for the best."

We arrived at the main road and began to walk down towards Aana. We had a first glimpse of the fjord and still I held Didrik by the hand. I was embarrassed that someone might see us. The air trembled with warmth. Blue dragonflies droned around us and over the gray and yellow gravel. Didrik's polished boots were already gray with the dust.

We approached the Carriage Stone. Once, many years before, two men had driven over the cliff at this very spot. They had been drinking and people said that when they were still in the town and climbing into their carriage, one of them had cried, "Now we'll drive straight to Hell!" And here at the precipice it had happened. When they plunged over, they took along with them the guard rail. Later it was replaced with an enormous round stone that people called the Carriage Stone.

Now a man stood beside the stone, out at the farthest edge of the cliff. Didrik pressed my hand hard and began to walk faster, and we were almost at the stone before I realized that it was father who stood there, with his back to us. He did not move until we stopped behind him.

"Is that you, Arnold?" Didrik's voice sounded strange. He raised his hand, as if he were about to strike. That was before father turned.

When I saw father's face, I knew that something was about to happen. He was changed, disfigured in a way. He seemed to be grimacing as he spoke to Didrik. "It was good of you to come," he said, and it seemed he was about to laugh. "I didn't dare do it alone."

He crossed to the opposite side of the road and stopped, motionless, his back to us. Suddenly he turned and stared straight ahead, past us. "Stay there!" he shouted. "Don't move!" Then he took off, racing towards the cliff.

Didrik reached him in one single bound. It was like seeing a man jump over a ditch. He held on to father's arm, and father tried to wrench himself free — I do not know how long they struggled. But suddenly father gave up, his head sank down on his breast, and he began to sob. Didrik led him across the road, over the drainage ditch and to a narrow, level place covered with bracken that was pale gray from the dust. He trampled the bracken down with his foot, and he helped father to get down on his knees, all the while talking to him gently, reassuringly, as if he were tying up a cow. Then he knelt next to father and began to pray. I had never before heard anyone pray like that. His voice was almost threatening. It surprised me that he was not more respectful. "If we stay here all day and all night," Didrik prayed, "You're not going to get away until You've helped. I'm not the right one to ask You for anything. You took Amalie and the little one away from me, and my heart was like ice. I hardened myself and turned against You in hatred. But when I stood on the edge of the abyss, then I asked You for mercy, and then You finally helped. And now I ask You to have mercy on Arnold."

Standing in the road, I saw them kneeling there in the trampled bracken. I saw the soles of their shoes. Didrik's were studded with shiny cleats and father had holes in his. Their backs seemed unnaturally huge and father's body shook with convulsive sobs. What did I feel? Disgust, horror, nausea.

I crossed over, and at the bend in the road stood Lars. He had hidden behind a boulder. He had followed father. I remember I thought, "We, too, should pray," and I approached him and wanted to take his arm, but he brushed me aside. Then he took off and disappeared into the brush.

Didrik still prayed. He repeated the same words over and over again, and I went further away to avoid hearing. Once I wandered far into the brush looking for Lars, and when I came back I heard Didrik still praying. Finally, I sank down behind a boulder some distance away, and I slept.

When I awoke I knew a peace such as I had never before experienced. Didrik was calling me. I came out on the road, and there they stood brushing off their clothing. Something had happened to father. He seemed calm. "Didrik will come home with us," he said in a low voice when he saw me.

But he was weak, and Didrik had to support him. They looked like a peculiar pair of lovers as they walked, arm in arm, down the hill.

I walked behind them at a slower pace and they were far ahead. I sat down at the edge of the road to wait for Lars. There was something I had to say to him, but I did not know what it was. He did not come.

Lars did not return home until almost eleven in the evening. By that time Didrik had gone. The minister had been there also. The mood was solemn, as if something dreadful had been overcome. Father was awake and spoke with mother while she packed his clothing. The next day she and the minister brought him to the asylum. He never again returned home and died fifteen years later, almost the same time that I was ordained.

Later I thought that it was perhaps on that day that I decided to become a clergyman. But I do not know. I am not at all sure about that. Such experiences are perhaps not so decisive as one believes. We know so little about what takes place inside of us; we hardly understand our own thoughts. We know that something exists within us against which we strive, something that fills us with uneasiness or with hope. And then, one day, it happens — one has an experience that clarifies everything that one has, for a long time, pondered. And at that point the decision has already been made and there is no turning back.

But I do know that something did happen to me that day. Something decisive. As if you rose up and left a place to which you would never return. It was a kind of choice, something that had to do with despair or hope, a yearning for something barely glimpsed. That day I did not completely understand. What burned inside of me was not that terrible moment when father raced towards the precipice, but the incomprehensible gladness I felt when I woke from sleep and heard Didrik calling me. It was not fear I remember best, but a sense of good fortune, a certainty that there was something that helped, someone who could help me overcome. That certainty was unshakable in the period of my life that followed — during middle school and later in my years as a student when I was often filled with doubt.

But at the time it happened, I naturally did not dream of becoming a minister. That was too distant. I did not even plan to attend high school although I knew that I was bright, that I was the best in my class. We were on public relief, and there was no talk of education. I had no concrete plans for what I would become when I grew up. I thought vaguely for a while of going to sea and later of entering an apprenticeship as a cooper — I wanted to be the best barrel maker in Aana.

But then something turned all my plans up-side-down. It was before summer vacation, the last year that Lars attended school. He was up at the teacher's desk getting a new pencil, and the teacher was beside himself with anger because Lars would not say 'thank you.' He held the pencil in front of Lars' face, and, over and over, he shouted that Lars should thank him. Lars stood there absolutely mute, and I realized that he would never give in. Without knowing what I was doing, I jumped up and shouted that he should let Lars be, and suddenly I heard myself shouting ugly, terrible words. The teacher stormed down through the rows of benches, his face gray, his mouth trembling, and he could not manage to speak. When he grabbed my arm to throw me out, I climbed up on my desk and began to scream. I do not know what happened, but the desk tipped and I tumbled down. The teacher fell, too. I saw his powerful body lunge forward. When he pulled himself up, I saw a glistening red drop on his forehead. It grew, and in the next moment there was a long stream of blood running down his cheek and onto his shirt. I took off, racing through the doors and out into the school yard. When I heard someone running after me, I leaped across the lawn into the outhouse, but there was no hiding place there, and I pressed down into the corner by the urinal. Someone came into the outhouse, and a minute later I felt someone touch my shoulder. When I looked up I was staring into Elna's face. Perhaps that was when it began between us.

"He was bleeding!"

"It serves him right," she said, and I remember that she dried my face with her hands. "I'm going to tell my father how horrible he was!"

I recall, too, her eyes. They were blue-gray with a glint of green. Her face was so full of life and excitement and anger and goodness.

I did not dare tell Didrik what had happened. When I arrived at school the next day, the teacher was wearing a bandage on his forehead. But he was calm, almost gentle. I interpreted that as a sign that my fate was sealed because I knew that he had been at the home of the minister, who was also superintendent of the school board. Perhaps they were planning to send me away to reform school? Or, perhaps, I would be whipped in front of the whole school? That was almost worse. Such a thing had happened in Aana some years earlier. The boy who had been punished — he had stolen a few pieces of colored chalk — went to sea when he finished school and swore that he would never return. He never did, either.

During recess Elna slipped me a letter. It was for mother from the minister.

We were asked to visit the minister that same evening. It was the first time I had been to the parsonage. It stood apart on a knoll beside the church. We walked with heavy step and mother held my hand tightly. Perhaps she was afraid that I would run off. But I was so exhausted that I barely managed to drag myself along the gravel path and up to the front doorway. I was bewildered, remorseful and terrified.

When we returned a half hour later I was even more confused, and now mother walked beside me and wept. I understood only vaguely what had happened.

The minister had first spoken about the incident at school. My behavior had been the height of folly, but the school teacher, as well, was to blame. The minister had investigated the case. His daughter, too, had told him about the unfair distribution of school supplies. He had spoken with the teacher. It would not happen again. We could count on that.

And then he began to talk about why he had asked us to come. Actually he would have preferred to wait until I finished school to tell us. As mother surely knew, Arnt Hansen, or Warehouse Arnt, as he was called, had, in his will, left his entire fortune to the community. He had, to be sure, no heirs. But there was an addition to his last testament. Eilif Grøtteland, he said, and looked straight at me, was to receive a certain sum for his education. If he wished to continue in school. And if he behaved himself properly. "It is a rather unusual proviso, but that is how it is."

He and the mayor were to execute the will to the best of their judgment. The rest of the money, and it was no insignificant sum, was supposed to go to a new old people's home and to the dredging of the river.

That evening still appears before me as unreal. An almost incomprehensible event had taken place. I have forgotten what I was thinking, but I remember well what happened: mother hobbling back and forth between the living room and the kitchen to fetch more coffee cups as the women in the neighborhood dropped in to hear the grand news. Off and on she wept. I have no idea where all her tears came from. "Your father should have seen this!" she repeated over and over. "I'll write to him this evening. He'll understand it, if they read it to him!"

I recall, as well, an evening six years later, the time when I told her that I had decided to become a minister. She did not speak. She looked at me with a strange light in her eyes, and then she struggled to the floor by the bench, and she whispered, "We should pray together."

She probably thought that I wanted that. But, seeing her crouching there, I was filled with repugnance, and I could not pray. "Get up, mother," I said. I still am ashamed that I could not overcome my aversion, that I could not, that one single time, forget myself and kneel at her side. But I could not. Lars was inside.

The following autumn I moved to the city and began my middle school studies. Later, when I finished high school and started my studies at the university, I returned home only during the summer vacation.

Mother wrote to me every week, and I faithfully answered her letters. During my last four years as a student I had a job as night clerk at a hotel, at this very hotel where we are now. The hotel was different then. Now everything has been modernized. Down at the reception desk I wrote letters to mother in the quiet hours after midnight, and the late hour probably influenced their contents. There must have been several hundred letters in all, but they are all gone. They were probably burned when the house in Aana was sold and the new owners moved in. I would have liked to read them again. Did something happen to me in those years, to my mind, to my inner life? I think about it every time I pass the reception desk downstairs. When did the change begin? It's no use to ask.

I've kept mother's letters, and I read them every now and again. There's nothing special about them — a few deeply pious thoughts that I later would use for my sermons, as clergymen often do.

They always closed with a verse from the Bible. She seldom read the Bible, so she had probably plucked, at random, a grain of wisdom from the book on the bureau. She wrote about ordinary, everyday occurrences, about what happened at home. She was filled with an indomitable courage — where did she find it? How did she manage to hold up against all the adversities she met in life?

Now things gradually improved for her. She was no longer on relief. My two sisters went to Stavanger and married well. Lars had a steady job with an automobile repair shop in the city, but he continued to live at home. Mother blossomed. They got new things for the house; I received a detailed report on everything. She also bought new clothing for herself, and twice a year she traveled to Kristiansand to visit father. After every trip, she wrote to me about how good he looked — fresh and tanned even though he seldom was outdoors. Sometimes he recognized her. There was always some mention in her letters about things that had to be done before father returned home.

But most of all she wrote about Lars and about how well life was going for him. He was serene and content, never touched liquor, and never went to dances. He kept to himself, staying, for the most part, in his room; the sofa and two chairs that father had inherited from his mother had been moved in there now.

I always longed for home. When Easter was over, I began to count the days until summer vacation. But what did I long for? I was increasingly a stranger in Aana. I stood out, probably because I was studying for the ministry. I had to be careful about what I said or did. There were other young people who were away at school: the mayor's daughter went to a teacher's college, and Jens Christian's son was planning to become a doctor. But it was different with them. They paid for their education themselves. I received money for my studies. Each month a postal money order came from the county treasurer, from Jens Christian.

It was, in fact, my own money, but I never thought of it that way. It seemed that it was the county that paid me, and I felt I had to tighten my belt an extra notch in order to avoid disappointing their expectations. I had to be the best, or, in any case, among the best. That is how I felt.

When I was home I sensed a mixture of envy and respect. It made me unsure of myself, particularly among those of my own age. But I was seldom with them. Nor did I have much desire to be. The young people were bored. They loitered in the streets or sneaked off to play cards behind the warehouses. On Saturday evenings they danced to phonograph records down on one of the wharves. And then their mothers would gossip about who had been there. The most hardened ones tapped kegs out in the fields and would return to Aana in the evening roaring drunk, cursing and hollering. They kept it up until they fell asleep at one or another house.

The young people from the evangelical church had more to do. Almost every year there was a revival meeting, and it was often the rowdiest who were the first to be saved. They held prayer meetings, witnessed, and organized music clubs. In the summer there was usually a trip down the fjord. Motorboats, filled with young people singing and playing guitars, chugged down the river.

A few times they asked me to join them. They apparently assumed that when I was at home I belonged among them. But the high-pitched emotional atmosphere and their sentimental Christianity made me uncomfortable. The prayer meetings were worst of all. I have always had an aversion to kneeling in the presence of others — except at the altar during services, of course.

Was that humility or was it pride? In any event, they interpreted it as pride. They thought that I considered myself too good to be with them. And perhaps they judged rightly.

I was most content when I was with Didrik at Hausebakken. The years passed. I worked, I read voraciously, and I yearned. I dreamed of the future. Among my fellow students I was one of the best.

Elna and I fell in love during my final year at the university. For me, life was still pointing towards new treasures and towards new and genuine happiness. I believed my life would continue like that, that things would always improve. Occasionally I experienced loneliness and doubt and despondency. But they never overwhelmed me. I had faith, hope and love; I had everything. That might sound like a platitude, but that is how it was. And then I met her.

It was like shaking an apple tree and the fruit showers down over you and you are amazed that, all along, it had been up there. Why did she choose me? And why did I not discover sooner that I loved her? I could not understand that. I had always known her. I had seen her every summer. Although her family had moved to Stavanger where her father had a new parish, they rented a house in Aana and would spend their summer vacation there. When Elna grew up she often came alone.

I talked to her off and on and saw her daily because her house lay across the river, only a short distance down from ours. But I did not particularly like her. I thought she was conceited. It irritated me that she always swam directly opposite our house, even though I knew she did it because the swimming was better there because of the shoals in front of her place. I did not like her to swim there because of the nervousness I felt when I saw her approach the river bank and undress in the alder thicket. When she finished bathing, she would sun herself on the boulders directly opposite our dock where I often sat and read with my feet dangling in the water.

I had a curious relationship with women. Girls, with their giggling and their physical presence, made me restless and excited — and a little frightened. Elna was one of them. But then there existed, in my imagination, other girls, or more accurately, one special girl, the one I would one day meet. She was a misty, insubstantial being. She, too, had a body, but it was made of another substance. It was something holy and sublime.

When Elna bathed, I marveled at how plump she was. She seemed almost skinny when she was dressed. But she was beautiful. I could not avoid noticing that. Her face, her blue-gray eyes with a touch of green in them — even then I often wondered about the word that could accurately describe the color of her eyes.

Something changed in her that last year. I thought it was because she had begun going out with Lars.

He, too, was different. We almost never spoke to each other in the years after father was sent to the asylum. But it became even worse after we grew up. When I would enter the kitchen, he would go to the bedroom, or he would leave the house and row out onto the fjord or ramble over the moors.

But now he was not so hostile as before. Neither was he as reserved. On occasion he whistled in the bedroom while he washed and dressed in the evening before he went out. When the weather was good, he and Elna went for long walks. And when it rained he crossed over to her place in the rowboat.

I was always restless when he was at Elna's in the evening. But it was worst of all when she was with him in our house. They sat inside in his bedroom and he showed her all the things he had collected: ants, snakes, beetles that he had preserved in alcohol, and all kinds of plants that I knew nothing about.

"What do you have against her?" mother asked, reproaching me. She noticed that when Elna came I always left.

Elna was always friendly to mother, but she had almost stopped talking to me, and it bothered me. Once, when I was walking up to Hausebakken I came upon her sitting by the pool in Tverrdalen and waiting for Lars. She barely nodded to me as I passed. I did not like them meeting there at my special place.

One Saturday evening before Saint John's Day, the church youth organization arranged the annual crabbing excursion down the fjord. I went along. Remarkably enough, so did Lars. Elna probably had talked him into it.

Falling in love is, to be sure, a banal thing for everyone except those who are experiencing it. I suppose I should describe this trip and what happened with the ironic condescension of an older man. But I cannot do that. Every time I think about it, I become emotional, even though I try to tell myself that what happened was, in fact, completely ordinary, something that happens to others a thousand times over.

We journeyed all the way out to the mouth of the fjord, to the farthest isles. It was one of those early summer days that begin cloudy in the morning and then turn marvelously clear. There was a view of the open sea, and a blue and golden stillness that slowly silvered as the sun sank. The sea, out there, was vast and incomprehensible. The long swells rose and fell almost imperceptibly against the mountain walls. The shriek of the gulls seemed a shrill warning that out there anything could happen. And there it did happen.

We landed on an island, made coffee, ate, sang, and waited for dusk so that we could begin to gather crabs. Elna and Lars kept to themselves. For a while they sat on the rocky beach. Then they rose and strolled further on. He reached his hand out to her when they climbed over a knoll. There they stood silhouetted against the sea and the pale shimmer of evening. They talked, stood facing each other, walked further, stopped again. And then they were gone.

I knew a loneliness that was doubly poignant because I suffered in the midst of a crowd that was laughing and singing while absolutely unaware of how I felt. I could no longer bear it and strolled down the beach away from Elna and Lars. There I sat for a long time and stared, dully, down into a tangle of sea kelp. The sublime quiet made the pain still worse. I could see inside myself with a clarity like that of the water. I dared admit what I had long known, that I loved Elna. Now I knew it. But now it was too late.

When I returned it was almost dark and the crabbing could begin. Lars and Elna had also returned, and with some others they stacked wood for a bonfire. Both of them were quiet, and I thought that it had surely happened between them.

We rowed out to a sheer cliff some distance from the beach. The crabs had climbed so high on the rock that we simply reached out and gathered them in with our hands. With my shoulder reaching out over the gunwale, I knelt and swept my arms down through the kelp where the hard, red backs of the crabs came into view. Every time I tossed another crab up into the boat, I saw the figures moving in the light from the bonfire on the island. I recognized Elna by her red sweater.

When we returned with our catch towards midnight, I felt certain that something had changed. Elna stared into the fire. Now and then she glanced over to Lars and I thought, "How happy she is." Lars was inordinately cheerful. He chattered and laughed. I had never seen him act like that before. When it was time to boil the crabs someone asked whether a crab or a lobster had the strongest claws.

Lars knew, of course; he knew everything about animal life. He picked up a large crab and held it upside down so that it stuck out its massive claw.

"Look!" he said and stuck his left thumb inside the pinchers. The crab immediately seized him.

A girl began to squeal and scream that he should stop. A boy tried to rip the crab away, but Lars shoved him aside. He stood there with his arms outstretched and the crab hanging by its claw.

Everyone watched, mesmerized, but Lars' face was expressionless. Then he turned the crab over on its back, broke off the claw and threw both it and the crab into the boiling pot.

"That one's for Elna!" he laughed.

She had paled, and she took his hand to look at it. There were two deep purple marks. When it was time to eat, he gave her that crab, but she would not take it.

Someone began to sing to lighten the moment, but the mood was spoiled. Lars was the only one who remained cheerful. He laughed and sang, and on the trip home he jumped across to a second motorboat that cruised right next to ours. There he began to balance on the gunwale until someone pulled him down into the boat.

I sat next to Elna in the bow of our boat, under a tarpaulin. How did we happen to be sitting next to each other? I do not know. It just seemed to happen. We sat pressed tightly together and, under the sailcloth, we felt each other's warmth. The rhythmic vibration of the hull nudged us closer together. I felt her touch and I grasped her hand. She let me hold it and then she squeezed it — at first lightly and then tighter. We leaned back and I thought how fortunate it was that the bow was so fashioned that our heads were pressed together. Her cheek touched mine. I whispered her name, but I do not know if she heard me over the drumming of the motor. But I heard my own name whispered, close to my ear, and I thought that now it was real, now she had said it with her own voice and not merely with the touch of her hand and of her warm body. Each movement was significant, something remarkable that we shared and that we both recognized.

In the darkness I could just make out her face and her glistening eyes. The sky was pale. A heron sailed high above with a slow beating of its wings. Perhaps it would fly out to the island. We slept and woke again. The mountains on the far side of the fjord had assumed the rosy hue of morning. The two boats drove close beside each other along the steep cliffs that lined the fjord. There was a hollow echo from the motors, but otherwise all was still. No one spoke. Lars, too, had become quiet. We did not think about him.

Father died a year later, almost to the day — on Friday, the 17th of June, three days before I was ordained in the cathedral in Oslo.

Elna phoned and told me that I had to come. She had found a job as a temporary teacher in the school in Aana and had lived there since the new year. She went together with Lars and mother to the hospital when they learned that father's death was approaching.

It was inopportune for me to come because I was deeply involved in my preparations for ordination. Three of us were to be ordained, and we were to play equal roles in the service. I was chosen to deliver the sermon. I had almost finished writing it when Elna's telephone call came. I had taken as my theme the fifty-third chapter of Isaiah, the fifth verse, "He was wounded for our transgressions, bruised for our iniquities; the punishment was laid upon him so that we should find peace, and through his wounds have we been healed."

As I sat in the night-train and reviewed my text, I added the fourth verse: "Our sickness has he taken upon himself and our suffering has he borne; but we considered him stricken, smitten of God and afflicted." It struck me as significant that I would be at my father's deathbed two days before I was to take my clerical vows. I thought about what had happened up by the Carriage Stone, and somehow it seemed that there was a connection between that and the text I had chosen. Father's long suffering and his impending death, my meeting Elna, the vows that I would soon take, all that which had happened to me in my life formed a pattern, like the pieces in a puzzle. A picture of me, as I was and as I was determined to be, took shape. Only later did I realize how preoccupied I was with myself at that moment, and how little I really thought about others.

It was raining when I stepped off the train in the morning, and I did not immediately recognize Elna. She waited in a raincoat and oilskins; her face was pale and drawn. She clung to me in the taxi out to the hospital and spoke hardly a word. I noticed how disappointed she was when I told her that I had to return to Oslo that same evening.

I had visited father, usually with mother, during every summer vacation. Lars never came along with us. He always went alone, and when he returned he was always reserved and barely answered when we asked him about father.

Now he and mother sat, one on either side of the bed. Mother stroked father's hand, his cheek, his arm — nervously and shyly as if she did not know where she should hold him. She moaned in a strange, whimpering tone. When she saw that I had come, she began to sob aloud. It was as if she had forced herself to hold back only so long, and now no longer had the strength. Lars sat motionless and did not take the hand I reached out to him. He gazed the entire time into father's face, watchful, as if he expected him to say something. He sat like that hour after hour, as long as I was there.

I could tell immediately that father's end was near. His breathing was heavy and now and then he made a deep, rattling noise. But he was not particularly changed — only a little heavier. His face retained his usual tan, and his hair was still dark and wavy, but it had lost some of its old shine. He did not recognize me.

A physician came in with a nurse, took father's pulse and left immediately. The nurse said we could get food in the cafeteria, but no one left. We sat silently hour after hour. Mother whimpered each time father made a sound. It had stopped raining, and when the sun came out in the afternoon, Elna closed the curtains so the light would not disturb us. A golden sheen lay over the room. Then the sun went down, and it was almost dark, but no one turned on the light.

I left for a moment, and when I returned, I realized that something was happening. From the bed came the persistent rattling that I would so often experience when, later, I sat with the dying. This was the first time. Lars had risen, and suddenly he shouted, sharply, piercingly, "He's dying! Don't do it father! Don't do it...!" I wanted to ring for the nurse, but I could not find the buzzer, and when I fumbled around the door frame for the light switch, Elna took my arm and held me back. Lars had thrown himself over the bed. He sobbed uncontrollably. Elna laid her hand on his shoulder and whispered his name. I had never loved her more than in that moment. I was so moved that I could not stop watching her, and only a little later did I discover that father was dead.

Lars stood up and studied father. Then he walked over to the window and opened the curtains. When he turned to us a little later, he was calm again. "Yes, yes," he said. His voice was firm and quiet. He left and did not return. Thirty minutes passed, an hour, the time approached when I had to go, and still Lars did not return. Later we learned that he had gone directly back to the hotel where they were staying.

Elna was ashen as we said good-bye to each other at the station. "Don't go," she whispered. "Stay with me tonight!" We had not been together, slept together, as they say it now, and when I held her in my arms and felt her body pressed against me, my desire for her was so strong that for one dizzying moment I was tempted to stay with her at the hotel. Everything else seemed remote and meaningless. But then the conductor politely took my arm and said that I had to board the train, that the doors were about to close.

By the time I was on the train and finally managed to open the window, we had already left the station, and I could no longer see her.

I have often wondered about that bright summer night when I sat by the train window staring into the billowing fog and the sun reddening the fir trees. Did I feel no anxiety? Did I have no premonition? None! I thought only of Elna. Soon I would see her again, hold her in my arms. She would be mine! I reached that weighty decision. We would wait no longer to give ourselves to each other. We would possess each other immediately. Anything else would be contrary to nature. Anything else would be sin. All night I thought about that. Although I had not slept for two days, I was wide awake. I think that was the happiest night of my life.

At the cathedral the next morning, I was dizzy with fatigue. But at the same time the world was illuminated with a sparkling clarity. I felt light, almost weightless. It was as if my aching body no longer belonged to me. I recall only dimly the ceremony itself: the whispered, nervous voices inside in the sacristy where we three who were to be ordained were waiting like anxious school boys. When the organ began the processional, I tried to remember Didrik, but I could not hold fast to his memory.

I had to steady myself as I climbed the stairs to the pulpit. As a precaution, I had brought along the text, but I did not need it. I knew my sermon by heart. Everything went perfectly. I knew it had from the warm handshakes of acquaintances and strangers alike when they came forward to congratulate me.

Afterwards, I went to dinner at the home of one of my fellow students. Red wine was served with the meal, and though I drank only one glass, it went to my head. Completely exhausted, I almost dozed off at the table. I decided to leave immediately. They all understood. They knew that I had lost my father, and I had not slept in two days.

I slept so soundly through the night that I barely made the morning train. And still I was not fully rested. On the return trip to Aana I sat, for the most part, in a corner of the compartment with a coat pulled over me, and I dozed and dreamed. I recall one of those dreams because it was so terrifying. I lay beside the open window in our room at home and stared down into the bottom of a muddy inlet cut off from the open sea by the stone wharves. The pool swarmed with frogs. Some crouched motionless on the bottom; others lay with their legs outstretched, like grotesque human fetuses. But most swam restlessly around and around, clung to each other and then swam further. In some places pairs of them lay motionless in each other's tight embrace, and elsewhere several were tangled into indissoluble knots of bodies, limbs, and blind eyes. I experienced a violent revulsion but, at the same time, an excitement, a yearning for them to move and to complete the act. I woke and slept again, and every time the same dream appeared. I knew I had dreamed it before, and I strove to recall when it was. Thus the entire journey alternated between the present horror of the dream and anticipatory terror in brief moments of wakefulness because I could not prevent the dream from recurring. Finally I forced myself to stay awake.

It was dark when I arrived at Aana, and I went directly to Elna's house. It was strange to go "home" on the other side of the river. I saw that a light burned in the window of the bedroom in my house, but at Elna's it was dark. The wind blew and it rained, and I thought that was why Elna had not met me at the bus. She knew that I would be coming.

She sat in the parlor and waited, in darkness, and when I came she got up to light the lamp. But I reached her first, embracing her, pressing her against me. She fought briefly to free herself and whispered that we had to talk, to discuss something. She repeated over and over that we had to talk, and all the time she struggled to get free. But I overwhelmed her with my caresses and my passionate words. My love for her swelled like a wave and made me invulnerable. I felt myself drunk with my own strength and little by little her body stopped resisting. She succumbed, clinging tightly to me when I carried her into her bedroom. When I had laid her on the bed and went to the window to close the curtains, I looked over towards our house. There was still a light in the bedroom and I could just make out Lars sitting at the window.

I had an appointment as chaplain in a fishing village in Finnmark, and Elna was enrolled in a teacher's college. We planned to marry the following year, when my appointment expired and I returned from Finnmark. But now we decided to marry immediately and travel north together. We arrived in the middle of August, still in time for the midnight sun.

The happy years of our lives began. Paradoxically they were the war years. And was it so remarkable that we were happy? We were young, we loved each other, and life's promises lay before us. Did not most people experience the war years in that way, as a happy time?

Is it not true that when we fight an enemy, when we are filled with hatred, and when our passions flare up, only then does life have meaning? Do not human beings then reach their full potential and become selfless, proud, and often filled with an inexplicable courage? Must we hate and fight in order to be truly human? Not everyone is like that. Some, of course, fight without hatred. They fight with love, and that, too, is inexplicable.

During the final war year that I was up in Finnmark, three Norwegian saboteurs were arrested by the Germans and executed. I was permitted to visit them during their last evening. One was a Christian, and the other two were communists, confirmed atheists. They did not hate. They were filled with love for life and for everything that they would be leaving behind. They had faith and hope in a future in which brotherhood and love would reign supreme, a future they, themselves, would never experience. I could not comprehend them, and I was filled with awe and wonder.

Later I thought about it. What if their dream should be fulfilled in a distant future? What will people be like then, when injustice and wrong are gone, when mankind lives and behaves as brothers? What will people fight for, look forward to? To whom shall they give thanks and whom shall they worship? How will they manage all of their happiness so that they do not burst from it? How shall they find relief from gladness when there is no more human suffering? Will happiness not become something cloying, unbearable? Can human beings live without gratitude? And can human suffering truly be overcome? After we have eaten of the tree of knowledge and know what we are? When those who follow after us shall also look into the eyes of their children and their beloved ones and know that one day they shall be dust, shall be nothing? Will not suffering, like a shadow, always follow us?

I can easily understand a person losing his faith. That is, after all, the natural course of things. But what I cannot understand, and shall never understand, that one can experience loss of faith as a liberation, yes, as a joy.

But perhaps happiness, too, is only an illusion, something from which we must free ourselves. I often provide counseling in divorce cases, and one reaction almost always is the same. Both parties deny the happiness they experienced together. They seem deathly afraid to admit it ever existed. Now that the marriage is over, it is important to convince themselves that it had all been a misunderstanding, and that the happiness, as well, had only been imagined.

Elna and I were happy in those years, ecstatically happy, even if the first period was filled with conflict. Elna was depressed and edgy; often she was apprehensive and unreasonable. But I told myself it was because she was pregnant — it was normal for a woman to act like that. It hurt me, though, and I regretted that I could not provide her with all the safety and comfort I would have liked. But my district was large, and I was always underway. When I recall those years I still feel seasick from the rocking of fishing boats in restless seas, and I recall the surf against dark mountains and endless days in blinding light.

It was autumn and the first months of winter, and Elna was constantly afraid that something would happen to me. She complained because I made her worry. "You can't love me when you want me to suffer so!" she said many times, and she even talked about going home to stay with her parents until our child was born.

But that changed after Lillian came. The birth came a little sooner than we thought, and I was out visiting the sick when it happened. When I pulled in at the wharf some fishermen were there, and one of them laughed and said that we had received a visitor. "Is it the bishop?" I asked, knowing that he would be coming one of these days. But from their laughter I realized what had happened, and I ran up the crag to the parsonage. Elna lay in bed. I still recall her words. "We must never leave here!" she said. I had received an offer to renew my appointment, and we were uncertain about what we should do. Now she was the one who did not want to leave. She was confident and calm. It was as if the fear had evaporated. The war came right after, and it became dangerous to travel in a sea with drifting mines and German patrol boats. But she was always filled with the same marvelous sense of confidence.

Only one thing really disturbed us — the letters from mother. She still wrote every week, but a kind of sadness had entered her letters. She still spoke of father. But now, as before, Lars was the favorite topic of her letters. She wrote about how kind and helpful he was. There was also something else in her letters that did not make sense. She complained about people's envy and all the groundless slander that was going around. Lars had moved away from home and had a new job.

Right to the very end, she defended Lars, just as she had always done when we were children. She died of pneumonia during the final year of the war, and when Ida wrote about the funeral, she also revealed the truth about Lars. He had become a Nazi and had gone over to the Germans.

When I read the letter to Elna, she was quiet, but I saw that the news upset her. "He is evil!" she said suddenly one day when we were talking about him, and I was surprised that she reacted so strongly. I tried mildly to defend him, talking about all he had gone through and how sensitive he was. I mentioned also how he had suffered the night father died. Once, near the end of the war, she sat at the table with Lillian, showing her photographs in an album. When Lillian pointed to a particular picture and asked who that was, Elna turned the page. When the child continued to fuss, Elna said it was Lars. "Why don't you say Uncle Lars?" Lillian asked. "Uncle Lars," Elna said quietly. When, a few days later, I looked at the album, I noticed that Lars' picture had been removed.

Then came the burning of Finnmark and the forced evacuation. Except for the church, every building in town was burned. We had two hours warning and could take with us only three suitcases of clothing and a little food. When we stood on deck in that dark December night and saw the bonfires flame up over the village and the church shining, white and inviolate among the devastation, I told Elna that we would return one day.

We did come back, many years later, in our old age. But everything had changed, and we, too, were not the same.

The journey south was long and difficult. The boat was crowded with forced evacuees and dysentery broke out on board. It was almost Christmas before we reached Aana and moved in with Didrik. It was the only place we could stay. The house Elna's family had rented was occupied by the owners and our house stood empty. Lars owned it now. He had not been home since mother's funeral, Didrik said. There were extra padlocks on the door, and the windows were covered with black-out curtains.

I was down there soon after we arrived. I had promised Lillian I would show it to her. As we gazed at the black windows, I felt a threatening and sinister presence, as if we were watched.

"Is this where Uncle Lars lives?" Lillian asked and squeezed my hand extra tight.

"He doesn't live here now."

"Maybe he's inside?"

We were, indeed, observed. As we walked back, I sensed people behind their curtains. Those we met greeted us with reserve and those I spoke with avoided all mention of the war, in order, I imagined, to avoid talking about Lars.

Both Elna and I felt like outsiders. We went down to Aana only to shop. But nevertheless that winter we were happy. We were together, and the unpleasantness and the reserve of others towards us made us feel even closer.

Lillian and Didrik became friends. She followed him everywhere and in the evening it was he who sat by her side until she fell asleep. "That such a thing should happen, that I should have people in the house, child!" he would say and shake his head as if he could not believe it. He had grown old in those years and no longer rang the church bells. After Christmas he had planned to move into an old folks' home. The cattle dealer who was to buy the livestock showed up some days after we arrived. Didrik and Lillian stood on the doorstep and received him, and when Didrik said that there was not, after all, going to be a sale, the man thought it was a trick to raise the price. He walked through the barn and the pig sty and kept making new offers. When he realized that Didrik was serious he grew angry and demanded payment for the truck he had rented.

One Saturday before Easter, we went down to Aana to shop. The day before there had been shooting and skirmishes out along the fjord. Commandos had landed from a submarine and Germans had been killed.

We were at the post office when the German car drove up and stopped outside the school, near the general store. When we approached, the road was barred and people were being ordered out of their houses. Jens Christian was arrested inside and his oldest son was also taken. Just after that the teacher was dragged out of his house. A German followed him, jabbing him with the butt of his rifle. The teacher bled from the mouth and was so badly beaten that he had to be lifted up into the truck. Just then, another car arrived and two SS officers and a man in civilian clothes jumped out. We were in the back of the crowd, up against the wall of the general store, and I did not, immediately, recognize Lars.

It had been quiet all the while. People watched, terrified, and only now and then could soft weeping and low murmuring be heard. But when Lars walked up to the group, it became as still as death. Why did he debase himself like that, I wondered. Or did he imagine this a high point in his life, a triumph over all the humiliation he had suffered? It was impossible to know what he was thinking. Calm, he nodded to acquaintances, and occasionally he said, "Good day," and mentioned a name.

When he saw us he pulled back slightly, and I saw that he reddened, and the white spots stood out on his cheeks. He nodded and smiled. "So here we have Eilif and Elna!" he said aloud and cleared a path through the crowd. Everyone moved aside and let him go forward. I held Lillian in my arms, and he studied her for a long time.

"So, this is Lillian. And this is how you look." He stroked her cheek, and she turned her face away. Then he walked quickly back to the car and immediately drove off.

During the evening of the 8th of May members of the Norwegian resistance came looking for Lars. They broke down the door and searched the house, and when they left they asked that they be informed if he turned up. Three days later he came. He must have arrived during the night, because when people got up in the morning, they saw him outside the house straightening things up and raking and burning the straw bedding and blackout curtains. He called to the coopers on one of the wharves and asked who had thrown the stone through his window. Afterwards he was at the general store buying glass and putty. At the same time he asked the clerk to telephone the sheriff and report his arrival. He asked if Jens Christian had come home yet. "He'll be back soon. I saw him a few days ago!" Lars said as he left.

When the sheriff and the men from the resistance arrived an hour later, Lars was replacing the broken glass. I was not there when he was taken, but they said he was perfectly calm and that he asked permission to finish mounting the windowpane.

The house stood abandoned for several years before it was sold. I was there the year after, and I could still see his fingerprints in the putty.

Towards the end of May I was appointed assistant minister in Oslo and we had to travel on two days notice. Shame and worry about Lars cast a shadow over our last days at Hausebakken. There were reports in the newspapers about the atrocities he had committed, but the worst of them were revealed only later, during the trial. Jens Christian and his son came home. They had both been tortured, but Lars had been present only as interpreter. The teacher went from prison directly to the hospital. He had been so maltreated that it was uncertain whether or not he would ever again be whole. In his case, Lars had personally participated.

On the 17th of May we attended the religious service in Aana and, afterwards, marched in the Independence Day parade. We did it for Lillian's sake. Ever since she was old enough to understand, we told her about the children's parade that always was part of the celebration of the 17th of May. We promised that she, too, would march when the war was over. The parade went from the school yard, over the bridge and farther on up the river. When we passed our house the procession grew absolutely still, and Lillian pointed and said, "There's Uncle Lars' house."

The last evening we walked around the farm yard and said good-bye to everything, to the sheep and lambs and cows that would be sold in the fall. Didrik led Lillian. I knew that he had something on his mind. In the evening when he sat by her bed and she cried because we were leaving, we heard him say that she should not cry because we would soon be coming back. He had decided that we were the ones who would have Hausebakken.

He had thought about it for a long time, he said a little later when the first overwhelming joy had abated and Lillian finally was asleep. He had already been to the sheriff and transferred the deed.

Life is strange. When Didrik had gone to his rest, Elna and I walked out through the farmyard and down to the stream. We had to see it again, and once more I told her the story of how I had first come there.

Lars' trial began the end of July and lasted two weeks. This period of my life appears before me as one of endless spiritual exhaustion and physical fatigue, and some of the blame lies in my lack of sleep. During the day I had to use all of my willpower to forget what happened in the courtroom, and at night I did not have the strength to push the thoughts away from me.

When I went to my office in the morning the name of my family glared out from the windows of the kiosks. There were pictures of him, of the instruments of torture, of the maltreated and butchered people. I forced myself to read the newspaper reports in order to be prepared when my turn came on the witness stand, but I never took my newspapers home.

Perhaps Elna read them anyway. I do not know. We never talked about what was happening. I had a heavy workload, and I was often away during the evenings. I was either in the office or visiting the sick and preparing children for confirmation. I seldom conducted services in the church. I did not have the strength to do that, and the parish minister was understanding. Whenever I introduced myself I noticed that people recognized my name.

Elna threw herself into her work at home. We had taken over a "German apartment," and it was absolutely filthy when we came. From the beginning she set to work scrubbing, painting, whitewashing the ceiling, and, yes, she even began to hang wallpaper. It seemed so senseless, because we were going to live there for only a few months. I had been given a chaplaincy in an inland community in Sørland, and we were to travel in October.

Up until the day we left, she continued working on the apartment. It was, perhaps, a kind of game that we both had tacitly agreed to play. But I saw how pale and devastated she was and how she clung to Lillian. Nights when we were in bed she snuggled up to me, and we would talk about the move and about Hausebakken and everything that should be done there. If an outsider had listened to us when we lay like that and whispered together, he would have thought we were very happy. Perhaps we were?

I was to testify in court on the final day of the trial, and I understood that the defense placed great weight on what I would say. It was the first time I was in the courtroom. I had imagined that I would be entering a passionate witches' cauldron in which my brother fought a furious battle over life and death, and it was a shock to experience the calm, relaxed mood before the hearing began. People stood in the corridor and quietly conversed. I heard two middle aged men, who, I later discovered, were judges, talk about the vacation they would take when the trial was over. The door to the courtroom opened and a functionary distributed papers.

When I was shown into the room where the witnesses waited, I saw a nurse bent over a man with crutches. It was the teacher. He was almost unrecognizable. His teeth had been knocked out, his hair was gray — he had become an old man. I recognized him only from his eyes. Filled with hatred, he stared at me when I reached out my hand and he acted as if he did not see it.

I heard the sounds of the courtroom: the shuffling when they all rose, the striking of the gavel when the court convened. Nothing happened. We just waited.

The waiting was the most painful of all. The entire time I fought with myself. I thought about my brother who would be sentenced to die and about the hate-filled cripple who wanted nothing but the chance to accuse him.

Lars sat with his defense attorney, to the right of the judge. He looked up when I entered, but he showed no anxiety. My presence seemed to make no impression at all on him. Even though I had, in fact, expected nothing else, his calm confused me. He was nicely dressed, handsome, apparently healthy and in good spirits.

In a half hour it was all over. They asked me a number of questions that I no longer remember — questions about our childhood and school days and our parents. Lars leafed through documents the entire time, making notes as if my testimony did not concern him. Was that in order to demonstrate his disdain? Sometimes he turned to his lawyer, who listened to me intently and who waved away Lars' whispered comments.

Only once did Lars react. It was when I described how Lars had taken care of father, following him and watching out for him. I also described the evening father died and how desperate Lars had been.

I had the best of intentions. I thought about all of those who now listened, judges, accusers, spectators, journalists; all demonstrated such hatred and disdain for Lars. I would show them that there existed in my brother a glimmer of humanity. He was not merely a monster.

Yet, even while I spoke, I realized that I wounded him deeply. Once he started to rise as if he intended to protest, but he sank back and remained seated, listening. He stared at me, and I felt, once more, my old fear of him.

All summer I tried to arrange a meeting with him, but he would not see me. I contacted his attorney, the director of the prison, and the prison chaplain. The answer was always the same. He had nothing to say to me.

The death sentence was delivered in the beginning of August. Some days later my sisters, Ingrid and Ida, came to Oslo to see him and to say good-bye. I was glad that they came then, before the Supreme Court had made its final review of the verdict. There was still hope. We behaved, in any case, as if we still clung to hope.

I met them at the station, and they began to sob as soon as they caught sight of me. They continued weeping in the taxi, and I had to speak sternly with them and insist that they control themselves out of respect for Elna and Lillian.

We had told Lillian that they were here to visit Uncle Lars who was sick. What else could we say? Lillian was happy that they had come, and she proudly showed them a picture that she had drawn for Uncle Lars and that she wanted Ingrid to take to him. Ida began to weep immediately when she saw it, and again we had to resort to lies. Auntie cried, we said, because she was sorry that Uncle Lars was sick. I had taken the day off, and all afternoon and on into the evening we acted out this macabre play. When it was time for Lillian to go to bed, Elna went in and lay down with her. My sisters and I remained seated in the parlor, the lights off, not speaking.

The next morning I took them to the prison. They were admitted immediately because I had spoken with the prison administration the day before and let them know about the visit. They were almost at the breaking point when I said good-bye to them in the lobby, but when they returned an hour later — I waited in a nearby cafe — they were composed, even optimistic. Lars was so calm, they said, and he was so pleased with Lillian's drawing. I asked them what he said and what they had talked about.

"Do you feel that he has repented for...?"

Ida interrupted me before I could finish. "He was perfectly calm. I believe he's handling it marvelously."

"And, really, it isn't even certain that...!" said Ingrid.

I received a confused account of the visit. They had discussed neither what had happened nor what would happen. They had talked about the old days, about things that had happened in their childhood, about people in Aana. "He was perfectly calm!" they both said again and again and chatted away with each other, anxious to remember their conversation with Lars. They were knit together with him in a camaraderie from which I was excluded. When I asked whether he had mentioned me, whether he wanted me to visit him, they looked at each other, embarrassed.

"I don't really remember," Ingrid said finally. "I don't believe he mentioned anything about that."

When I wanted to call a cab, they once more glanced at each other with embarrassment. "Since we are, in any case, in Oslo now," Ingrid said and blushed. It seemed they wanted to shop a little and see the city. They wanted to visit the parliament building and the National Theater, the palace — one of the guards came from the town where Ingrid lived, and she asked to begin with a visit to the palace. We had lunch in the Theater Cafe, visited the Steen and Strøm department store. All day I trailed after them. Watching them stand at the counter, excited and busy with choosing cloth, counting money, and looking over their ration cards, I felt a sense of unreality and, also, of horror. Not that I criticized them, but I could not believe that they could behave in that way after their farewell with *him*. What mysterious power he had over people. I was afraid to meet him and suffered because he would not see me.

They left that same evening. The days and weeks went by, and sometimes I thought that nothing would happen, that it would pass.

The 29th of September, two days after the Supreme Court had confirmed the judgment, Lars' attorney called and said that I could come to the prison at eleven that evening. The execution would take place the same night.

I could not tell Elna. If she knew what would happen that night she would not be able to stay alone. I had to bear it alone. When everything was over it would be easier. So I thought. Perhaps that evening I took the first decisive step down the long road of secrecy and lies that lay before us. Perhaps our lives would have been different if we had, then and there, spoken openly with each other. Later it is easy to recognize the fatal errors one makes, often because of love and a misplaced sense of consideration.

I was composed when I returned home for dinner at four, but perhaps precisely that hard-won composure aroused Elna's suspicion. I noticed that she watched me when I played with Lillian. At seven I embraced Elna in the foyer and mentioned that probably I would be late getting home. She seemed to want to hold me back, to tell me something, but I avoided her by talking about the details of our move. We were supposed to leave in a few days.

I went to my office, locked the door behind me and disconnected the telephone. I did not turn on the light, because, as rector, my office adjoined the minister's, and I did not want him to see me there and, perhaps, stop by. Could he, possibly, help me, advise me? I rejected the thought immediately. I had to bear this alone. Only God could help.

I was to meet Lars in two hours, and I pulled my chair up to the window and tried to decide what to do.

But it was useless. I had no idea what to say to him. I did not even know what to bring with me.

It was a clear autumn evening, cold and quiet. I looked up at the starry sky. Perhaps Lars, at this very moment, stared up at the stars through his cell window. What was he thinking? What did he feel? Had he had a change of heart? Was he as unrepentant as ever, or was his soul bowed in remorse and, face to face as he was with the inevitable, did he pray for grace?

My clerical shawl hung on a peg. I folded it in my bag, together with the case containing the consecrated bread and wine of the Eucharist. But when, in the darkness, I felt the soft fabric of the shawl, I saw his face before me, full of hatred and disdain, and I returned it to its place. Finally I took with me only the Eucharist, the Bible and a pack of cigarettes.

What had I expected? Almost anything! Except what happened. Even before I sat down, he confronted me, and he was cruel and merciless. Was that because he wanted to put me at a disadvantage right from the start? I had not come to argue with him. I argued with myself. He would die, I would live, and I could do nothing to change that. But I was defeated from the moment the guard unlocked the cell door and let me enter. Lars was calmly waiting when I came in. I am the one who suffers, not he, I thought as I reached my hand out to him. To my surprise, he took my hand and pressed it briefly. His touch caught me off guard. I had had a vague idea that he would bear some sign of what would happen, that he would be different. But he was so absolutely the same — his face, his eyes, the small wart on his neck, the somewhat boyish way he shook back his hair. His warm hand reminded me of his body under the blanket in our bedroom — he was always warm. I believe it was at that moment, when he touched me, that I realized what would happen.

"So, now you see how I live!"

"Lars," I said, and tried to steady my voice. He continued to smile.

"This is what death row looks like," he said. "Would you like to look around?" He gazed along the walls. I had barely noticed the cell window, the bed, the table. We stood on either side of it. Now I glanced around in order to gain time, and I noticed that his eyes were fixed on something behind me, on the wall by the door. I turned. There hung Lillian's drawing.

I had seen it the evening before Ingrid and Ida visited him, and I knew that they had brought it along. But I had only given it a casual glance. I had not thought about what it portrayed. When I saw it again on the bare cell wall it made a powerful impression on me. Not only because Lillian had done it. It was the drawing itself. It was utterly simple. The lower half of the page was covered with a blue sea, and on the upper half was an enormous rainbow against a dark sky. Two gulls glided over the sea. As I stared at the drawing, my back to him, he spoke the words.

"I believe," he said softly, "I believe that Lillian is my daughter."

I heard the words, but I immediately forgot them. I find it incomprehensible that I managed to do that. I shoved them out of my consciousness during our conversation, as one lays aside an unopened letter. I remember only one dizzy moment when I thought, "Later. Now it is Lars' time. Help me, God, to forget."

"Yes, she draws well," I said and turned back to him. I noticed an uncertainty in his eyes, but he regained his composure quickly.

"Sit down," he said with authority, and pointed to a chair. I fumbled with the bag that I still held in my hand, and he smiled again. "Is that your equipment?" and, as if he guessed my thoughts, he added, "Did you also bring your clerical shawl, your vestments?"

"No. Only the Eucharist."

"A minister was here at eight. He also had his equipment, but I said no thanks. I'm having a meal at one, and then I want to eat alone."

"Lars," I said as quietly as I could. "We have to talk. You're going to die in a few hours!" It was terrible to blurt out these words, but I had no choice.

He snapped his fingers, as if he had suddenly thought of something, as if, perhaps, he had not heard what I said. "Or maybe you're hungry, maybe you'd like to eat with me? Salmon! Wouldn't that be something? A last meal, two brothers!"

"Lars!" I interrupted, and I saw that I angered him.

"Will you stop repeating my name all the time!"

"I will not do that," I answered. "I know that you hate me. I don't know why, and I won't ask. That's unimportant now. I admit that I feel helpless, but nevertheless there is only one thing I can ask — Is there anything I can do to help you?" He did not answer and I said, "There is only One who can help."

"You mean that we should talk about God?"

"About God's love and the hope for eternity."

I had to gather myself forcibly together to say that, and I was prepared to have him answer me with scorn, but he nodded thoughtfully.

"We should talk about that. About hope. That's why I asked you to come."

"That's why you asked me to come?"

"I want you to listen to me."

I quietly waited. Let him speak, I thought. Don't say a word! But it was obvious that he did not know how to begin. There was a long silence. I fought back the memory of the words that he had spoken when I had looked at the drawing. I fixed my gaze on a package of cigarettes on the table.

"Do you want to smoke?" he asked with a nod. I lit a cigarette, and when I saw that there were only three left, I bent down to my bag.

"I've brought along a pack..."

But he waved it away. "I stopped smoking some days ago."

He began to talk about Ida and Ingrid's visit. They also had brought cigarettes. "It's apparently a common belief that those under sentence of death have a special need for cigarettes. That's what people usually bring along."

"Cigarettes can work as a sedative," I said, and I realized how banal the discussion was becoming.

"I don't need a sedative."

"They meant well."

"Yes, they meant well, and it was pleasant to have them visit. When they finally stopped weeping."

"I spoke with them on the phone today. They love you so much." I hoped that by saying this I could lead into what I wanted to talk about — about love, God's love. But it was useless. His inhuman quiet was unshakeable.

"Oh yes, they love me," he said. The word "love" apparently offended him. "And when this is over, they will love me even more. In a few years they will sit over their coffee cups and calmly discuss their brother and the last time they saw him. I could not speak sensibly with them. For that I needed you!"

He studied me through the smoke, and I put out the cigarette. "Yes?"

"First a few practical things. My insect collection. It's inside a milk tub, wrapped in oilskins. I buried it in the yard, next to the gooseberry bush, the night before I was arrested. I want Lillian to have it!"

He is saying this to provoke me, I thought. I nodded, although I knew that I would never dig it up.

"And then there is the house. Is it sold?"

"I don't know."

"It will be sold, of course. Everything I owned has been confiscated. Nothing will remain after me, unfortunately."

"That doesn't mean anything," I cried. I was about to say "now," but I stopped myself.

He responded, annoyed, "Nonsense! Obviously it means something. I would have liked Lillian to have it. Now she has to satisfy herself with...." He considered for a long time, as if choosing his words with care, and he seemed somewhat dissatisfied when he finally said,

"Yes, she'll have to content herself with what I say, with what I am. I want you to tell her that."

I knew that I would never fulfill his wish, but I answered calmly. I had decided to get up and leave. It was useless. "What should I tell her?"

"That I was not afraid."

"I'll tell her that," I answered, relieved that that was all. But then I realized what his words meant. He spoke the truth. He knew no fear. It dawned on me that his suffering was of another magnitude than my own. He sat before me, a lost human being. Was he human any longer? He knew no fear.

To this very day I believe he could read the thoughts of others. Perhaps that was what gave him such power over people. He added, immediately, "Naturally, I feel a certain physical fear when I think about the details. But, nevertheless, I know that that is only something transitory, that it will pass. Tomorrow it will be over."

"Everyone is afraid to die," I said. "We require a hope."

"I have a hope," he answered softly, and I understood both from his tone and from the light in his eyes that it was this he wanted to talk about. "I have a hope that is stronger than any other, because I know, with absolute certainty, that it is the only thing that will be fulfilled. Everything else is nonsense, fantasy. I know what fear is, and I know how to overcome it. Because I am gambling on a certainty. The only wish that can be fulfilled!"

He studied me for a long time. "With all your belief in God, you are afraid to die." His stare forced me to look away. "Don't deny it!"

"I don't deny it. I am afraid to die. But I have a hope."

"What does that mean, to hope? It means that you do not know."

"Yes, that's true," I said softly.

"The difference between you and me is that my hope is stronger. Because I know."

"What can you hope for?" I cried. "You will die, Lars. You must recognize that. You will die tonight!"

But he continued. "The difference between you and me is that you will drag along for a while longer with your fear. Because what do you think about, you and all the others?" He nodded towards the cell window. "I've heard the din of their celebrations down in the city. But what do they think about in the midst of their noisy festivities in the name of peace and victory? And that one over there! What does he think?" Again he nodded, this time in the direction of the open cell door. The guard sat just outside. I could see his legs and feet. He pulled them in. We both noticed that, and, for a moment, it was quiet. Through the stillness we heard the sounds in the building — the ringing of a distant bell, a door being opened. "And the director of the prison? And those who now wait with their rifles, and are scared shitless because of what they will be doing — what, in your opinion, will they be thinking about when they squeeze the trigger? They will be thinking about exactly the same thing as you and all the others, those who are born and those who will be born, are thinking. They will think:

this is me; it will happen to me! Are they fortunate? Do they have hope? What a pitiful hope."

"They have something to believe in."

"What do they believe in? In lies! That death is something that will strike everyone except themselves. *That* they believe in!"

He sat a while and caught his breath, as if now everything had been said. Then, unexpectedly, he lit a cigarette.

"One should not be excessively consistent," he said quietly. It was as if what he had said would become truer through this little touch of humanity. He took a few deep drags, put out the cigarette, and then he said, "Now it's your turn to talk. Begin!"

I thought for a long time because I knew that my words would be of vital importance.

"You're right," I said finally.

He looked at me, as if he did not like my answer.

"The world is filled with fear and suffering," I said. "But I believe the suffering can be a path leading home. It can show us the way to truth."

"I, too, believe that," he responded dryly. I did not understand what he meant, and he said, slowly and with emphasis on every word, "Suffering forces us to look into the eyes of truth."

"What is the truth for you?"

"The truth, the only truth, for me and for everyone else, is that thing which is going to happen to me tonight."

"Lars!" I cried, but he gestured me away with his hand.

"Only when one realizes the consequences of that, can one overcome that which you call suffering. I don't understand why everyone does not see that. It seems so simple. The suffering of this world can only be overcome when there is no longer anyone who can experience it."

I did not understand what he meant, and I tried to repeat the sentence aloud, but he interrupted me again. "When there is no longer anyone who can experience it, when we are gone, all of us, when there is no longer anyone who can feel or think! Is it not precisely this thinking, this feeling that is the source of all evil? The great misfortune in the world. Imagine that there rose up a new race of beings who could feel like us, think like us, think, in fact, better than us, beings who increased and began to multiply. Do you believe we would consider that a good thing? No, we would see it as a misfortune and would do our utmost to exterminate the pack of them! These cancer cells! And that is what we are — cancer cells!"

He sat for a long time and breathed deeply. Something alien had entered his voice when he continued. "Do you remember the birch tree outside the house of father's mother in Lista? The one with all the knots? It's still there. I saw it a year ago when we passed through on a raid. She once said, 'My body, too, is like that. Full of knots!' Now she is gone. The knots are gone. Everything is gone! Now the sea beats in over the rolling stones, the gulls fly in over the land in the darkness. It's good to remember that. That is what I will think about tonight. I will think that some day everything will be like that. The waves will roll in from the sea and the gulls will shriek in the wind — and no one will hear them. The tides will roll in and roll out again, and no generations will follow. That is what I have been doing — bringing things back to where they should be, to the silence. It has just begun. Someday it will all be still."

He looked at the drawing behind me. "Lillian — she will understand that. Already she understands that perfectly. The sea, the gulls, and a rainbow that no one can see. That is what I have been privileged to be part of. That is what you will tell her. You will be my witness."

I stood up. "She is not yours. She is mine!"

Again he was calm. "Mine and yours, let's say she is ours. No one knows for sure."

"I will not tell her that."

"You will, all right."

"No."

"Will you keep that knowledge to yourself? For the rest of your life? Keep silence? You are too cowardly. Too weak." His whisper was filled with hatred. "You are like father!"

I went to the door, and he called, "Your briefcase!" and when I turned to take it, he stood by the cell window with his back to me.

"Good-bye, Lars."

He did not answer. I cannot remember how I got out of the building. Nor do I recall what I did afterwards when I stumbled through the quiet streets that night. I only know that it was cold and that I was freezing. Towards one o'clock I was back outside the prison, on a side street by the great iron door. I knew that inside he sat at his last meal, alone — and I felt hungry. To deaden my hunger, I took out the pack of cigarettes that I had planned to give him, and when I fumbled in my bag and touched the case containing the Eucharist and the Bible, I felt ashamed. An hour later the iron door opened and there was the sound of a motor inside the courtyard. Two policemen on motorcycles drove out, followed by a large private car and then a closed police car. They drove right past me, but I could see nothing through the back window. I waited until the sound of the motors faded, and then I ran towards home. I had to talk to her now, immediately. But when I stood outside the apartment house and saw the lights in the windows, I turned and began to walk back towards downtown. Once, in the course of the night, I found myself outside the church office, and right afterwards I stood outside the minister's home, and I thought I might wake him up, but I did not. All the time I thought about what Lars had said and about what was now happening to him. I did not dare pray because I did not know what to pray for, but I clung to a Bible verse and I repeated it again and again. It was from the First Epistle of John. "He who says that he loves God and hates his brother, he is a liar, for if he does not love his brother, whom he has seen, how can he love God, whom he has not seen?"

He is my brother, I thought, but the word rose up before me like a wall. If only he were not my brother, if he were anyone else at all, but not my brother!

I returned to the apartment house and crept in under the stairs on the first floor. As morning approached, I thought, "Now it has happened, and now I will go up and talk to her." But I did not dare. "She is mine," I thought. "He will never take her away from me!"

The street door opened, and I heard steps above me, ascending the stairs, immediately followed by a sharp clanging from the mailboxes — the morning newspapers had arrived. When I reached our apartment, I saw a newspaper on the neighbor's doormat, and I picked it up. There was a short notice on the front page saying that Lars had been executed.

I had barely touched the key to the lock, when the door was opened. I handed the paper to Elna without a word. She glanced at it, let it fall to the floor and embraced me. I began to cry, and shortly afterwards Lillian came running out. Elna lifted her up and, with the child between us, we held each other. "It is over now," I thought. "I have to forget what he said."

But how could I forget his words? I could not, on my own, dispel the doubt that he had sowed in my soul. There was only one possibility: I could ask God to drive away the evil thoughts that threatened to overwhelm me. Prayer and work could save me, I often told myself, and I did both of them, but I made one grave error. I avoided the company of others. I decided to bear it alone. To whom could I open my heart? With whom could I share the terrible secret I carried? I had only one single wish: to forget it, to wipe it out of my mind.

Perhaps it would have been different if I had received a parish in another town, another district. But I had come back to my beginnings, to my own home. My parish lay inland, but only sixty kilometers from Aana. It was an isolated, closed community. Lars had been there on his raids, and everyone knew that I was his brother.

I was shaken by what had happened, and, therefore, I was vulnerable. But I must not be unfair to my parishioners. They never mentioned Lars. Nor did they give me any reason to believe that he figured significantly in our relationship. It was me they watched, me they tried — and I did not pass their test.

The very first week that we were there the council chairman of the evangelical community meeting house came to the parsonage to welcome me. He was a friendly man, a farmer and a road construction worker, and he greeted me warmly and with kindness. As he was leaving, he asked if I would come to the meeting house and speak to them the following evening. I said I would — and I went. I have forgotten the subject of my sermon, but I recall distinctly what happened afterwards. When I had finished speaking, the chairman stood up and thanked me, and then, looking me straight in the eye, he said, "And now the pastor will lead us in prayer!" We stood facing each other, and I recognized in him the politician, the clever tactician. He wanted to test me in the presence of everyone, to see whether I was one of them, one of the genuinely "saved," or whether I was the other kind of minister, the arrogant, superficial kind who only kneeled at the altar. How revolting it was, I thought, that they should use prayer against me. Was it only a question of my pride? I thought about my mother that time in the kitchen. It would have been a betrayal of her if I now gave in. When they knelt, I remained standing, and when they were all down on their knees, I read the "Our Father" — and I left.

That was my first meeting with them. A state of war existed between us from the first moment, and it separated me from those who should have been close. I longed for fellowship and brotherhood, but I shunned those who would have given it to me. I chose to be solitary.

It grew worse as time went by. My relationship with my clerical colleagues in my parish district cooled. Once I signed a protest against nuclear weapons, and I noticed immediately, from their attitude towards me, that I should not have done that. My action offended them. The bishop spoke to me about it in a friendly way. He did not criticize me, but he mentioned that a minister had to be extremely careful that he not be used politically.

I had never been involved in politics. It did not come naturally to me. I scorned the politics I encountered in the church, in the congregation, among my colleagues. But I was concerned with the question of nuclear disarmament. Lars and what he had said in his cell the night he died about stillness and annihilation were always in my thoughts. To fight against that was to fight against him and against his words.

But in the eyes of the church that was politics. More and more I saw in the church's position a betrayal of the message it should deliver. Where was its love and its concern for suffering in the world? Where did the church stand in the battle against evil and sin? And where were the sinners? I met none! I met fine, noble people, but no sinners.

I knew my moral stance was just. But what I did not understand was that my righteous wrath was a two-edged sword — it struck at me and closed my heart and isolated me. I fought on two fronts, and the worst battle

was that which I waged against myself, the struggle to
forget what had happened. It was the same as that time,
long ago, when I tended the cabbage field. Every time a
memory shot up, I asked God to take the evil thought
away from me, and I told myself, "Now you have con-
quered. Now it is forgotten!"

And I did manage to forget for weeks and even
months. But the thoughts returned and always with
greater strength. Shadows of doubt came over me when
I was least prepared – at a school board meeting, during
a visit to the sick, in the pulpit when I looked down on
Elna and Lillian. Was Lillian my child? And who, in fact,
was Elna? Did I know her?

At home we seldom spoke of religious matters and
never of Elna's spiritual life. A wall separated us. Did she
believe in God? I did not know. She participated in my
work, attending funerals and services at the home for
the aged. She read the manuscripts of my sermons and
proffered praise or criticism that I almost invariably
heeded. I was deeply dependent on her. When, on rare
occasions, she was not present in church, I felt insecure.

She and Lillian had their permanent place in the
church – the third row, to the left of the center aisle.
She always sat with bowed head and listened when I
spoke. Only a few times did she glance up as if I had said
something that astonished her, and then I immediately
wondered what it could have been. And at once the
thoughts overwhelmed me. What was the truth? What
had happened? Had it happened the night father died,
in the hotel room, the night I sat in the train and was
utterly happy? Often I had to pause, take out my hand-
kerchief or leaf through the text in order to master my

emotions. But then, when I closed my eyes in prayer, the scene appeared once more before my eyes: Lars crouched over the bed weeping, Elna's gentleness as she stroked his hair, and finally — the hotel room.

Although I thought it could not be true, doubt always echoed within me: If Lillian were my child, why had we not had other children?

Afterwards, I would be exhausted and therefore my behavior at the dinner table was probably forced. "What happened during the sermon? Did you lose the thread of your argument?" Elna would ask. She teased, and there was often laughter and joking about "the thread of papa's argument" that Lillian should try to follow.

Indeed, the bantering during those festive Sunday dinners would usually end in a wild gaiety that would sweep away all the nagging doubt. In those happy hours I thought, we must talk this out. I always imagined that it would happen at Hausebakken, where Didrik had lived.

In the first years we were often at Hausebakken. I had the path widened so that we could drive in all the way, and in the winter I had an arrangement with the road maintenance people to clear away the snow.

When we climbed out of the car in the courtyard, we always stopped and listened to the quiet. Lillian had a ritual — she would thank the farm for the happy times we had spent when last we had been there. She charged through the shed door, into the empty barn, up the ladder to the hayloft, and out the loft door. Elna and I had to wait until she had made her rounds, thanking the farm.

"Life is so good to us!" Elna would say, taking my hand. I never knew if she realized that she repeated herself. "Life is so good to us!" she said many times. I always listened to her tone, and then I noticed that she said it less often, and finally, she no longer said it. "We must talk," I thought.

One day during our summer vacation, Lillian and I were down by the brook. I had fashioned a water wheel under the hollow wooden gutter, and when I turned the water on, the wheel began to turn and, at once, a rainbow appeared in the cloud of spray that hung above the paddles. "See the rainbow!" Lillian cried, and in that instant, I thought about the drawing she had made for Lars. I stared at her, saw his face before me, and immediately drove it out of my mind.

"It doesn't go away!" Lillian cried.

"No, our rainbow will always shine," Elna said. She stood close behind me, but I had not noticed her arrival. Why did I think her words banal and sentimental? People must be permitted to be sentimental occasionally. That is the way people are, I thought, ashamed, but I pulled away when Elna laid her hand on my shoulder.

"Are you afraid of me?" she asked.

"I was just startled."

"You never did that before."

"What have I never done before?" I asked, irritated, but my tone was conciliatory. "What have I never done before, dearest?"

"I don't know," she said sadly. "Somehow you stiffened when I touched you."

"Nonsense," I answered cheerfully. "Come and sit down and see the rainbow we've made." And again I thought about the drawing.

"We have to think about her," she said after a while.

"What do you mean?"

Lillian stood out in the brook and watched us, listening to what we said. I saw how the light in her face was extinguished. Elna reached out to play with her, but she did not want to play. She climbed up and pressed our heads together so that we would give each other a hug. We sat close together, and Lillian crept up on our laps.

"We have to talk," I said.

Elna only nodded and Lillian asked, afraid, "What will you talk about?"

"About Uncle Lars." I forced myself to say that, and immediately I was terrified because of what I had done. Now there was no return.

We spent the entire day together. We walked down through Tverrdalen, all the way to the pool, and in the afternoon we picked blueberries in the fields. We spoke quietly about everyday things. When we had eaten supper, I went in and put Lillian to bed while Elna cleared the table. I heard the clattering as she washed the dishes in the kitchen. When she was finished, she walked into the parlor and waited. I felt a growing fear for what might happen, but I was determined to talk about it as soon as Lillian had fallen asleep.

While I sat by her bed and held the child's hand as she slowly drifted into sleep, I realized that I did not dare talk to Elna. I did not want to know the truth.

Night was falling, and I could not see Elna's face as I entered the parlor, but I sensed the tension behind her quiet voice.

"Shall we walk, or stay here?"

"We'll stay here," I said, and I sat beside her on the bench. And as quietly as I could I began to speak about what had happened in the cell and what Lars had said about his yearning for death and for emptiness. "He made me doubt," I said, and, listening to my words, I realized I spoke the truth! The thoughts that he had sowed within me had begun to take root. But at the same time, in the midst of my doubt, I observed her.

"Is that what has tormented you all this time?" she asked, marveling. It struck me that she seemed relieved. Was she relieved that the cause of my torment was other than she feared?

Unobserved, Lillian had come into the parlor. She stood in the doorway and watched us for a while, and then she left without saying a word. We did not light the lamp, but remained sitting side by side, the darkness thickening around us. We were silent and distant from each other. What, after all, could we talk about?

So, we do not even have Hausebakken, I realized.

Had I begun to doubt? Was I losing my faith? I told myself that it could not be true. What did Lars' evil beliefs have to do with my relationship with God? I forced myself to remember the Carriage Stone and what had happened there. There was One who was stronger than death and hatred and wickedness. Every time I fought my way through, I felt stronger in my faith.

But was I not lying to myself? Was it not true that the more I thought about Lars' relationship to Elna and Lillian, the less strength I had to resist the evil thoughts that he had sowed within me? Something was happening to me without my realizing it.

It began with weariness and despondency over my lack of achievement. Especially when working on my sermons, I was overwhelmed by despair.

Writing had never come easily. I had always worked painstakingly over my sermons. But in the past I had looked forward to the hours when, locked in my office, I would work on them.

Now I hated the chore. I put it off as long as possible. It was not that I was in doubt over what I should say or that I lacked ideas, but, rather, that I found it so difficult to formulate my thoughts – to find the right words.

When I would write something down, I would immediately begin to question it. I would stare at the words thinking, "So, this is what you intend to say! These are your words! But do they represent you?" I began to compare my sermons with what others had written on the same text. I reviewed what I had studied, in order to make certain that my sermons conformed to orthodox theological interpretation. And then doubt sprang up. I would erase what I had written – and change it and rewrite it.

For hours I would pace the floor in the spacious room on the second floor that I used as my office. It seemed too narrow. I had to go outside. I began to take long walks. Only after I had walked for an hour's time did the oppressive feelings that had gripped me begin to abate.

I almost always went to the same place. I walked up the valley as far as a certain cattle pen near a farm. There I turned and continued on home — quickly, eagerly. It was as if the physical exercise enlivened my thoughts and once more they had meaning. I stopped, took out a pad and pencil and made notes, walked further, stopped once more. When I arrived home, I went directly up to my office and began to work. It was as if my faith and my salvation depended on my being able to write, to formulate what I had been thinking. Only when it was on paper did I believe in it.

But with increasing frequency I simply could not write it down, and then everything fell apart. I would begin anew. On Saturday evenings I often struggled late into the night and continued early Sunday morning until a half hour before the service was to begin.

When, exhausted because I had not slept, I stood in the pulpit and looked out over the scattered congregation in the pews, I knew the bitter pleasure of self-pity. If they only knew what this sermon had cost me!

What did they know about the price of faith? About what it cost to sit beside a deathbed and speak of God's grace and of the eternal hope? To stand beside the grave and say the last words — "And from dust thou shalt rise again" — to look into the eyes of those who suffered and to see myself, to know that the words were not merely sounding brass and clanging cymbals!

That, to be sure, was a mystery — incomprehensible. When I gazed out over the congregation and studied them one after another, I wondered whether they really did believe. They seemed offended if anyone dared to doubt the incomprehensible. They treated wonder and mystery as something obvious, a kind of inheritance that they claimed. Was it not true, perhaps, that they thought of the church as a spiritual supermarket where, each week, they picked up comfort and assurance, in the same way that they collected their social security from the town treasury? What did they expect from me? That I should fill them with Christianity and old-fashioned morality? So that they would have sufficient spiritual nourishment to last until the following Sunday?

Often my musings shocked me. I listened to myself and I thought, "Do I love these people?"

I spoke of love, but bitterness grew within me. I spoke of hope, but doubt steadily darkened my intelligence. That which, earlier, had assuredly been joyous certainty, had now become something I could only struggle to approach. I had become an actor.

I knew where it was taking me, and I also knew how to be saved – I had to overcome my pride, place everything in God's hands and pray for mercy. But I was unable to fight against bitterness. Though I did not want it, I sought it. I did not have the power to choose.

The poison that Lars had sowed took root in me. Constantly I placed new pieces into this evil jigsaw puzzle. Recollections sprang up – of things that had happened, words that had been said. It always ended in that darkest moment in my life – the night my father died.

Often I paced my office at night thinking about how Elna had destroyed everything for me. I charged her not merely with her faithlessness. She had killed something within me. She had turned my heart into stone. I hurled my mute accusations at her. "You, you, you...!" I whispered and listened for her approach. Let her come so I can say it to her face. Why did she not come if she had nothing to hide?

Shaking with shame, I listened in the deathly still house, and when she did not appear I marched up and down on the floor, noisily, so that she would hear me. A few times I also heard her steps, on the stairs, along the hallway to the door — and there she stopped. Thus we stood, each on our own side of the locked door and listened. When I finally opened the door and saw her drawn, exhausted face I said, with wonder, "My dear, is that you? I thought I heard someone."

"What is wrong with you?" she asked sometimes. "Why don't you come and lie down?"

"I'm working."

So the years passed. How did we endure it? The incomprehensible is, to be sure, that we could hide it. We lived in a small community, among people who were close to us — I as pastor, she as school teacher. When Lillian was older, Elna substituted at first and later had a permanent position. We took part in meetings, marriages, funerals; and also, occasionally, in social gatherings. She still sat in the third pew during church services, and she read my manuscripts as before; I could not avoid that. I was never afraid to show them to her; they were not dangerous. There stood the word of God, of grace and salvation, of the victorious Christ who had overcome death and become a living hope. But never was there a word about our own need, our own dead hope. They were faultless formulations, these sermons that were so splendid that, I thought, they deserved a place in an anthology.

When I returned home in the evening after a meeting or a visit to the sick, I often stopped down in the street. The parsonage stood before me: a pretty, white house at the end of a row of birches. A window in the first floor was lit. Elna sat behind it in a wing chair and read. She read constantly. I saw Lillian in the next room. She, also, sat and read. Soon the light would be lit in my office window, and when the people of the community passed by they would look up and think, "Life is so good to them!"

During our first summer, before we went to Finnmark, Elna and I had camped in the area. I often thought about that when I stood there below the row of birches. We had pitched our tent on the mountainside across the valley. Early in the morning, when the mist lay over the lake and over the river, we lay on our stomachs in the opening of the tent and looked out over the valley, with the church and the parsonage on the other side of the river. I remember Elna said, "Imagine if some day we were to live there."

If, then, we could have looked into the future, seen the parsonage with the light in the windows, would she not have said, "Life is so good because we have that to look forward to." And if we could have seen into the bedroom when the light was out, when we lay close together and whispered to each other, "Darling," then we would have said, "Our dreams are fulfilled."

For that, too, happened. Year in and year out we lived together as man and wife. Right up until the time that I was no longer able. It went that far. Why am I doing this, I would think as I drew her close and whispered empty words. I did not dare admit the truth — that our love was dead and that our marriage was a ruin, hidden under the poisonous brambles of pretension. I did not dare to tear them aside. That would mean confrontation, reckoning — truth. Even when we embraced I saw them before me — her and Lars. In the end that bitter realization became my only pleasure.

But there was someone from whom we could not hide the truth — Lillian. She said nothing, did not object, never complained. But I noticed sometimes that she watched us, wondering, helpless. Only once do I remember that she mentioned it. "Everything is so sad," she said. That was all.

That was the day before she left home. She had completed high school and was about to begin her studies at the School of Fine and Applied Arts in Oslo. We had decided to visit Hausebakken during her final days with us. When she climbed out of the car in the courtyard she just stood there, and I asked, "Aren't you going to thank the farm for the last time?" All the years she was growing up she had continued with her tradition. Grown up? She was still only a child, I thought, as I watched her shuffle towards the barn. She walked so slowly. A long time passed before she emerged, once more, from the hayloft. Afterwards she wandered around the yard while we carried in the luggage. When I came out a while later she was sitting by the brook. I saw the strange jerking motion of her back, and I thought that she was crying. I walked down and sat beside her and put my arm on her shoulder. A little later

Elna came and sat at her other side. That was when she said, "Everything is so sad."

We stayed for a long time watching the water in the pool. We had installed a pump for running water and the old wooden gutter was gone. It lay in the alder thicket, rotted and broken in two.

"We'll certainly come back again next summer," Elna said.

"Yes."

"And then we'll make a new gutter and a new water wheel... and make a rainbow."

I remembered what had happened years before and I thought about the drawing. But this time I was not upset. I experienced only sadness and a vain realization that it was too late. That was the first time that the phrase sank into me with the decisiveness of a stone falling through water. Was it, indeed, too late? Or could that hour by the brook have been a final chance that passed and was lost and that I only later realized was the missed opportunity? I constantly wonder about that — perhaps it was not too late, perhaps it all would have been different if, then, we had seized the opportunity and talked.

The house was empty after Lillian left. We listened to the quiet she left behind, and we watched each other. When we talked it was about the Christmas vacation when she was to come home. When Christmas finally arrived, we did our utmost. Elna and I almost managed to be loving to each other. We invited friends, went for hikes, and during the main church service she and Elna sat in their permanent place. But something distant had come over Lillian, and when, on the third of January, we stood on the platform at the station and I saw her waving out the window until the train disappeared into the tunnel, I had a feeling that this was a farewell.

When the summer vacation, which we yearned for, finally arrived — then it was too late. Then she was already on the way into a darkness in which there was no rainbow.

I met her at the station, and we drove directly to Hausebakken. When we climbed out of the car in the courtyard, I was anxious to see if she would perform her ritual of thanks to the farm for our previous visit. But she merely dragged her phonograph out of the trunk and began to play records. It was disturbing to hear that ugly music there in that courtyard.

In the days that followed Lillian grew more and more restless. I urged her to hike with me, but she was not interested, and the times she did come along, I realized it was merely to satisfy me. She left after one week. She was going to meet a girlfriend in Oslo, she said, but she would return soon. We tried to convince her to invite her girlfriend to Hausebakken, but it was no use. She wanted to leave.

For the first time I discovered that she lied. She said that the friend had no telephone. The day before, she had gone back with me to the parsonage because I had to teach a confirmation class, and there I heard her telephoning her friend. I did not dare confront her with the lie. I thought about my own dubious relationship with truth and I was silent.

A week passed, and she did not return. We called Elna's cousin in Oslo and asked her to visit Lillian's student apartment. But she was not there. Then Elna went to Oslo while I moved back to the parsonage to be near the telephone. The third evening Elna called — from Copenhagen.

"I've found her," she said, and her voice was calm, but filled with pain.

"Has something happened?"

"We'll take tomorrow's ferry home. We can talk about it when we see you."

When I stood on the wharf the next morning and watched them walk down the gangplank, I saw that something was wrong. I gave Lillian a hug, and we silently crossed over to the car. Earlier she would always climb in the front seat next to me, but now she sat in the back with Elna. Perhaps she has been seasick, I thought when I saw her pale, wasted face in the rear view mirror. When we had left the city behind, Elna said, "Lillian is a little upset. Her girlfriend had some problems and she began to use...." She did not speak of drugs. It was unnecessary. I had long suspected it. "She convinced Lillian to try it, too," Elna added. "But we'll get over that. Isn't that so, Lillian?"

A week later she left again. We had begun to hope. She seemed to be coming around, and she looked better. We had begun painting the house, and she helped. One day Elna and I went down to Aana to shop, and when we came home she was gone. We drove directly to the railroad station, but she was not there, and no one at the station had seen her. "She must have hitchhiked!" Elna said, and we drove down to the main south road and then further east. Pale, Elna sat beside me, and each time a hitchhiker appeared on the horizon, she half rose out of her seat. "My poor child!" she whispered when she saw that it was not Lillian. "She's my child, too!" I cried, and she glanced at me and was silent.

Hour after hour we sat side by side in silence. It was midsummer — bright sunshine, happy people. I knew that it was useless, but we kept driving anyway.

"How long should we continue?" I asked finally.

"We'll drive all the way to Oslo if we have to."

"I doubt that we'll find her there."

"We'll try, in any case."

"And if she telephones home and no one is there to take the call?"

We did not turn back until after we had passed Arendal. On the return trip we stopped at every roadside restaurant and cafe, but hope sank as we neared home. Elna wept without a sound. "She has no money. She'll end up on the streets."

I was silent about what I knew. When I bought gas I discovered a note in my wallet. "Forgive me, papa." That was all. Five hundred crowns were missing. The words wounded me like a knife. Why did she not curse me? It would have been easier to bear. But never a complaint, never a grumbling word. Only her horribly hurt gaze. And then this, "Forgive me, papa." I kept her note with me. When I was alone, I often took it out and studied the childish handwriting. The last time I looked at it was on the way back from Copenhagen two years later.

For two days I had made the rounds of that narcotic hell down there. I searched for her with the help of a social worker from the Norwegian consulate. I knew him because I had been there twice before to bring Lillian home, and he, too, knew who she was. We were in contact with several other young addicts. They had seen her some days before, but did not know where she was now. There was a place out by Nørrebro, a condemned tenement — more they did not know.

As it turned out, I found her totally by accident. It was midday, and I was alone, searching up and down the side streets of Nørrebro. A young girl passed me on the sidewalk, and I recognized the sweet smell of hash. It reminded me of sickly sweet incense. I had learned to recognize it. When I turned, she disappeared into a gateway, and I followed her. Inside the courtyard, I saw that the inner apartments were empty. The naked windows gaped at me. The girl disappeared into one of the stairwells, and I reached her again on the fourth floor where a door opened to an apartment. She hurried inside, and a man tried to shove me away when I ran after her. They did not answer when I asked about Lillian.

I left them and walked down a long corridor. It was indescribable in there, disgusting and confined and filled with a pervasive and horrible stench. Garbage and mattresses lay everywhere. Perhaps the water was turned off, because when I passed the toilet, it stank of urine and excrement. In a back room the windows were covered with newspapers, and in the darkness I could just make out young people sitting on the floor. They stared at me dully when I came over to see if Lillian was among them.

I found her in the innermost room, on a mattress. It was dark, and I had to light a match. In the brief moment before the match burned out, I thought it was not she. But when I tore the blanket from the window,

I recognized her. Her face was yellow and skeletal. I shouted and shook her, but she did not react. When I took her hand I saw that her left arm was swollen and infected. She breathed slightly, and after a while she opened her eyes and gazed at me. Her pupils were shrunken into small, dark pinpoints. I could not tell if she recognized me or if it was fear that I read in her glance. She stared at me as if at a stranger. Then she closed her eyes and began to toss her head back and forth.

"I'll be right back!" I shouted in her ear and ran out. It took perhaps fifteen minutes before I contacted the emergency ambulance service, because when I finally reached a telephone booth I had forgotten the street number of the building and I had to run back to check. Then the entrance was locked, and I was forced to break the glass in the door to open it from the inside. In the meantime, the young people had vanished and only Lillian was left. She lay on the mattress, unconscious. Her jeans were pulled down and she was naked. It was the first time I had seen her as a woman. When I tried to shake her awake, I discovered a needle between the wall and the mattress. Had she done that to escape me again, I thought, while I tried to pull up her pants. But I had to give that up, and finally I sat on the floor and held her hand while I waited for the ambulance. She died that evening without regaining consciousness.

I telephoned Elna an hour later. When I told her what had happened, she did not answer. I heard only her breathing. I shouted into the receiver, again and again, but she said nothing.

I took the Copenhagen-Oslo ferry home the next day and watched from the upper deck when the hearse arrived with the coffin. It was transferred on board through a midship cargo door. When I went down to the hold, the coffin was already in the refrigerated store-room. I wanted to go in and sit with her, but one of the crew asked me, in a friendly way, to leave. So I went to the upper deck and found a chair.

It was one of those unforgettable August days: warm, mirror-still, the passage of the ship creating the only slight breeze as we travelled up through Øresund. A hydrofoil passed, and a sharp-sterned sailboat, its white sail flapping violently back and forth when the waves from our ship reached it. The sailboat continued to rock for a long time. When it finally was still, it was far astern. Out in the Kattegat we met long sea swells, but they were so gentle that I did not feel their move-ment under the ship. Then the sun went down and night began to fall, but it was still warm. I put my hand on the deck and the planking was warm. And down below she is freezing, I thought and went down and sat outside the locked door of the refrigerator. A sailor came in. He muttered when he saw me, but he left quickly. When I came up on deck some hours later it was night and a star-filled heaven arched over the dark sea.

In that way we journeyed home.

I had been given two months leave; my assistant conducted the funeral. Elna and I held hands when he threw the earth into the open grave. Then evening came, and we finally talked. I listened while Elna told her story, and I thought how utterly inconsequential it was. It was as I had thought. They had been together in the hotel the night father died. He had pleaded, and she had been weak. At that time she still cared for him. Only later did she understand that he had wanted to revenge himself on me. She did not know if he was Lillian's father.

"It's probable," I said. "We've had no other children."

"No. None."

Three days later she left. I was not surprised because she had left the parlor door open so that I would hear her telephone conversation with her cousin in Oslo. Her cousin, a teacher, had found her a position. They would live together temporarily.

"I think it's best for both of us," she said while we waited in the station. She reached her hand out to me. "Farewell, Eilif."

"You'll come back," I said without taking her hand, and she turned away. When the train disappeared into the tunnel, I climbed into my car and drove to Hausebakken. I had plenty of time. No one was waiting for me.

For the next three weeks I sat on the stone steps, watched the driveway and waited for her return. I made no effort to analyze my situation. I listened. Memories streamed through me, disconnected. Everything had become vague, indistinct. Even the memory of Lillian was unclear. I had to force myself to remember her face. I listened to the murmur of the brook, to the wind, hoping, thus, to hear my own inner voice. But there was no voice. There was silence and emptiness. And in those silent weeks, it happened. Something was gone. Each day was like a new farewell. But what was absent? I did not ask. I sat in the silence and pondered what was happening within me.

One afternoon I walked up the main road to the Carriage Stone. I had never told Elna what had happened there. When we, on rare occasions, went down to Aana, we drove past it without pausing. Several years had passed since we were last there.

Weeds covered everything and I did not recognize it. I had to search to find once more the stone where I had crouched and listened to father and Didrik. When I finally thought I had found it, I stopped, uncertain whether this was the right place. When I crossed over to the precipice, crows flew up from the rock-strewn slope, and the stench choked me. The city Department of Sanitation had begun to use the slope as a dump, and it was covered with garbage, tin cans and plastic shopping bags. I must be getting farsighted, I thought, when I discovered that I could read the text on the cardboard cartons. Was it really no higher than this? Was this the precipice?

When I returned home a while later, I felt relieved because I finally had reached my decision. For twenty years I had often considered the possibility that one day I would cease being a minister. I had always envisioned this moment with horror. Now, when the decision was finally made, I was astonished at how easy it had been. "Why did I not do it before?" I asked aloud, and I stopped and listened. I felt no pain — in fact, the pain was gone, I realized with wonder.

As I neared Hausebakken a taxi drove towards me. The driver, as he passed, touched his hand to his cap.

He lived in our town, next door to the parsonage, and I thought of the note I had written when I was last there to pick up my mail. "Welcome home," I had said. "You will find me at Hausebakken."

When I reached Hausebakken I saw Elna sitting on the steps, waiting. She stood up and approached. We met by the bridge and reached out our hands to each other.

We stood there a while, gazing down into the brook. I thought of how the water streamed down through Tverrdalen, down to the river and out into the fjord.

I felt a profound peace.

"I could not do it," she said quietly.

"We'll manage as best we can," I answered.

Later we strolled over to the steps, sat down, and I told her that I had decided to give up the ministry.

For a long time she did not answer.

"Are you sure about it?"

"Absolutely certain."

Then she nodded and said that she agreed; she also agreed that we should sell Hausebakken. We talked for a while about how that would best be arranged. A lawyer in town could handle the sale. Everything was to be sold as is. In the early evening, we immediately began packing. The work was quickly done. We took only clothing, books, and papers and managed to fit everything into the car.

When we were ready, she went outside and sat in the car while I walked from room to room checking that nothing had been forgotten. On the shelf over Lillian's bed were a few small things — an unusual rock, pine cones, a juniper root.

"Are you sure you haven't left anything behind?" I asked when I came out to the car. She shook her head. Then we drove off. In the evening I wrote a letter to the bishop. I asked to be relieved of my duties for reasons of health.

A new period began in our lives. Because Elna found a permanent teaching position in Kristiansand, we moved there, and I worked as a part-time instructor in religion.

We had a new apartment, new friends. The first anniversary of Lillian's death, the 4th of August, we spent in the south of France, at a campground with a view of the Mediterranean. With the settlement from Hausebakken we had purchased a camper, and all winter we had planned this trip. The year after, we went to Finnmark, and we visited the village where we had lived during the first years of our marriage. There was still no road connection there, and we had for our visit only the half hour that the local steamer lay at dock.

Things went better than expected, far better. When we sat in the parlor in the evening, Elna with a novel and I with a map and tourist brochures, I often thought that I was, to be sure, content. I said it aloud, now and then, "Life is so good to us!" and she always looked up from her book and nodded.

One summer, on our way home from Vestland, I suggested that we drive down to Lista. Elna was tired and stayed in the car when we finally reached the place where my grandmother's house had stood. It was difficult to find, because a gas station was there now and the road had been rerouted. But what Lars had described was accurate. The birch still stood there, behind the car wash. The tree was exactly as before. Apparently, it had not grown during all those years. The weather was as it had been when I was there the first time — thin clouds, creating dark patches of shade over the sea, and a glimmer of sunlight on the wet and stony beach. I walked down to the shore, I watched the waves that rolled in over the stones and the kelp, and I felt a kind of suspense. Now, I thought, I would finally find the response to the question, the only question I wanted answered. I thought of what Lars had said in his cell the night of his execution. It had burned itself into my brain. I could recreate it, in my memory, word for word, as if the tips of my fingers were touching an old, familiar scar. When I reached the beach I closed my eyes, and I saw him before me, as alive as if he stood there in the flesh. Was I frightened? Was I anxious?

I waited for a long time until I was certain that I did not deceive myself. But I knew that it was true: I felt nothing. He had said that which now I, myself, knew — that I would die. It was nothing to be afraid of, because it was nothing, nothing at all.

Now I realized, as well, that I had known that for a long time — ever since that night I sat out on the deck, that clear, starry night when Lillian and I journeyed home on the ferry.

I gazed out over the sea and cried, "So, you have won, Lars!" Even these words evoked no fear in me, but as I walked back to the car it seemed that I had behaved foolishly.

Yes, I had behaved foolishly. What do we human beings understand? We believe we know the truth about ourselves. And that, too, is like foam on the surface of the ocean.

Some months later I could have stood at the same spot and shouted over the sea that he had not won, but mine would not have been a shout of triumph, but one of terror in the face of death. I had imagined that I no longer feared death, that, in fact, I looked forward to it. But I had not met it. Death was, for me, always the death of others, never my own. Now I felt its chill breath. And I trembled in terror.

I do not know how or when it started. It must have been a while after the trip to Lista. I began to wonder why I was always so tired. It reminded me somewhat of the weariness I had experienced after Lars died. When I was young.

Now I was older, and though I did not feel old and thought I was unchanged, I attributed my fatigue to my age. When I looked at Elna, though, I thought of old age. She had grown thinner and wrinkled. It was as if the skin covering her face and neck was too large for her. When, rarely, we hiked together, she was quickly out of breath. I walked some steps ahead of her and constantly had to wait. We are the same age, I thought, irritated, and I suggested that she begin a gymnastics program. I myself went twice a week to the gym, and I continued to take long walks as I had done in the old days. I had a fixed goal in those walks; a beaver pond four kilometers outside the city. I always sat there a while and watched the huge pile of branches and hoped that someday I would see the beaver. I never saw it. I continued to walk to this spot, but now I often stopped halfway, convinced that there was really no reason to go any further.

When I returned home I was tired, but I felt no need for sleep. Sometimes I lay awake all night, and occasionally I went into the bathroom and examined my body in the mirror.

That is how it began, with a persistent inner fatigue. "I don't understand why I'm so tired," I said a few times in the beginning, and Elna always replied, "I'm tired, too."

Her response irritated me, and I stopped talking about it. I hid my condition from her. The months passed, and I grew neither better nor worse, except that mornings I often felt nauseous.

Even that I managed to hide. When I vomited in the bathroom, I turned on the shower so that she would not hear it. When, afterwards, I studied my face in the mirror, I noticed, with horror, how I had changed. Finally I no longer dared to look at myself in the mirror. I avoided it, just as I avoided looking at Elna. At the same time, I wanted her to notice what was happening to me. It wounded me that she only thought about herself.

When she complained of fatigue, I put her off, saying, "Take a leave of absence or a trip. Rest!" But when, finally, she followed my advice and announced that she would visit her cousin in Oslo, I regretted my suggestion. She went off, I thought bitterly, even though she knew that I was sick. She left me alone with my fear.

Many believe that sickness brings people together, but often the absolute opposite is true. It separates them, makes them strangers to each other, drives them into loneliness. I discovered that in those months when fear, in the end, overwhelmed me and I thought of nothing else.

A week after Elna left, I visited the doctor. He examined me thoroughly, and I was prepared for the worst. Nevertheless, it was a blow when he, in his dry, businesslike way, suggested I have an examination at a hospital.

"Is it cancer?"

"It need not be that at all," he said evasively. "But it's certainly best to be on the safe side."

He filled out a form that I was to deliver to the hospital, and I stared numbly at the word, *suspicio*. It chilled me to the bone.

I felt a little better when the hospital examination was over.

The doctor spoke openly and factually, and with some flimsy optimism. "It doesn't look so bad, but everything depends on the lab tests."

I talked to Elna on the telephone in the evening, but I told her nothing. Two days later I called the hospital to learn the results. The physician's voice, coming over the phone, frightened me. He was hesitant, evasive, it was still too early to say anything for sure, but there was something on the X-rays.... I was to meet him the next morning.

The rest of that day I stayed in the apartment, unable to get a grip on myself. I tried to eat, but I immediately vomited up the food. Elna had promised to call in the evening, and I was uncertain of what I would say to her. When the telephone rang at eight, I did not dare pick it up.

It rang several times in the course of the evening, but I remained motionless, sitting there in the chair, staring at the telephone.

Utterly exhausted, I finally realized how sick I was. The mere thought of leaving that chair seemed impossible. It was March and the evening sky was clear and light. March, April, May..., I thought. How long? I did not fall asleep until late into the night, and when I woke at about eight, it was like struggling to the surface from the bottom of the sea. Fear overwhelmed me even before I was awake. I wanted to sleep, sleep, sleep....

I feared death and clutched at life. I tried to convince myself that this was absurd. What was life really worth? Was it not merely an evil time of waiting, a time of foreboding in the face of the inevitable? Again I thought about what Lars had said. I thought of him when the nurse led me down the corridors to the doctor's office. This was truth, reality. Everything else was only lies and illusions.

The nurse called my name through the door and I heard the doctor's tired voice inside saying, "Let him come in." He sat there talking into a tape recorder. I realized that he must be making a report about the patient who had been there before me. He mentioned blood count, the patient's general condition, and the date for the next checkup. Each time he completed a sentence, he turned off the recorder and scratched his head with the microphone. The gesture seemed so careless, as if he were ordering groceries from the supermarket.

"And so we have Grøtteland here. How are you?" Before I managed to answer, he began to write something down in a red pad. "Yes, yes, we'll proceed as agreed," he said to the waiting nurse, and then, with a nod, he disappeared through the door.

The nurse turned to me with a friendly smile. "Now I'll take you there," she said.

At once I knew what was about to happen. I was to be admitted immediately. I had considered the possibility on the way to the hospital, and had decided to ask for a postponement. Now I contemplated my decision as we walked down the corridors, and I experienced the decay within me, the darkness that before I had not dared fully realize. I would never leave here. I would sleep, sleep... On my bedside table at home lay a pillbox. Once, in the course of the night, I had fumbled in the darkness and felt its small round surface with my fingers, but I had immediately pulled my hand away. Now I regretted that I had thrown away my chance.

"I would like to go home first," I said, as I followed her.

She stopped and looked at me. "Home?"

"I am going to be admitted, am I not?"

"We hope that won't be necessary," she responded, and I thought about hopeless cases, about how people are sent home to die. As a minister, I had often visited such patients.

The X-ray department was full of people, and the nurse had to fetch a chair for me from the hallway. The waiting room was large and airy, with doors leading into small rooms, like dressing rooms in a public bath. At regular intervals a nurse appeared and called a name, and immediately someone rose and disappeared into one of the rooms.

I noticed a young man. He seemed almost at the breaking point each time the nurse appeared. When his name was finally called, he stood up, waiting motionless, pale like a corpse. His face grew flaming red when, a moment later, the nurse said that he should proceed. Without a word he marched forward, and when someone called to him that he had forgotten something, he turned, picked up his glasses from the table and nodded bitterly. I saw tears stream down his cheeks. Others seemed calmer. An old man worked on a crossword puzzle, and when he was told it was his turn, he took his time and asked a passing nurse for permission to tear the page with the crossword out of the magazine.

Before this, I often felt sorry for old people. Now I thought how misplaced my sympathy was. They were alive. They had held onto life. Perhaps the old, too, some time in their lives, had confronted the inevitable, but they had overcome death and destruction. In fact they, the chosen, deserved to be envied.

Then it was my turn. I was numb when I stood in the narrow changing room. An orange dressing gown hung there, and I took it quickly in order to avoid seeing my body in the mirror.

A nurse summoned me. She was a tall, ungainly woman, and in the half light of the X-ray room, with its blue bulb over the machine, her face seemed unpleasant. Her voice seemed full of resentment when she told me to stand in front of the screen. With a harsh tug on my hips she turned me around and pressed my body in against the green plate. I knew that this was the end. Now I had completed my journey. In the next instant these rays would light up my insides and reveal death's embryo growing in me. The nurse distanced herself, and then a sharp voice sounded from the next room. "Breathe deeply and hold your breath."

With a struggle, I managed to follow the order. A weak, buzzing noise sounded and immediately after came the voice — "Take another deep breath!"

"Now it's over," I thought numbly, as once more I dressed. I shivered with cold and nausea and had to use the toilet in the corridor. When, later, I returned to the waiting room, I passed an open door and I heard a familiar voice. My doctor was inside with other men in white jackets. They stood in front of a rack on which hung several large X-rays. The light was turned off and on, and at once the pale contours of a skeleton appeared on the negatives.

A while later my name was called. I mechanically followed the nurse who brought me back to the doctor. Once more I stood in front of the office door. I heard the rustling of a newspaper inside. The doctor let it carelessly fall to the floor when I entered. Without introduction, and in an irritated tone, as if he were now sorry to see me, he said, "Yes, yes, Grøtteland, now we've looked into every nook and cranny. You're perfectly fit."

When I emerged into the spring sunshine and the fresh air, I was dizzy. The chill that had earlier made my body feel alien, melted into such swelling warmth that, at first, I thought I had a fever. I simply could not comprehend that the doctor had said that I was healthy, that I would live. I stared, perplexed, at the piece of paper I held in my hand. It was the prescription the doctor had given me. Apparently, I was somewhat anemic and had a touch of intestinal catarrh.

When I try to recall what happened in those hours I always arrive at a point of unreality, as if it were someone else who experienced it. Everything appears unreal, but, at the same time, curiously clear: the faces, the simply equipped doctor's office, the remarks that were made, my own thoughts. Not once had I thought of Elna.

It was only when I stopped and studied the prescription that I recalled that she also was anemic. Some days after she left she had mentioned, on the telephone, that she had visited a doctor. Now I felt a great tenderness towards her.

I took a taxi home and immediately tried to reach her cousin's apartment, but no one answered the phone. I called several times during the afternoon.

Towards nine in the evening her cousin telephoned to tell me that Elna had been admitted to the Radium Hospital that same morning. She was operated on the following day. That was her first operation.

The minister stopped speaking. He began to pace from the bathroom door to the window where he turned quickly as if there were something in the street that he did not want to see.

"I never thought about her," he whispered and stopped in front of the bed. Earlier he had been lying on top of the spread — his glance moved over the impression of his body, from the foot to the head of the bed. "I never considered her. It was always me: my own loneliness, my own fear. Only then did I finally realize what she must have suffered in all those years, and how terrible life must have been for her. Finally I understood. But it was too late."

He stopped and his voice changed. "No, no, that's not true. I *had* thought about her. I did think about her. But I had never identified with her suffering and made it my own. Now I could do that, but now it was too late. I could identify with her need. But I could not help. What help could I give?"

He sat on the bed, bent over, his hands dangling loosely between his knees. Olav Klungland noticed how Grøtteland stared at his hands. The minister looked up and said: "It was like that the other time, too. I sat on the stone steps at Hausebakken and helplessly stared at my hands." He held them up and studied them. "What help could I give her?" he repeated. "I could hold her hand, beg for forgiveness, find books for her to read, give her whatever she needed! But what did she need? What she really needed I could not give her. I could not give her hope. She had hope after the first operation. I saw how hope, like the light of a candle, was kindled in her eyes. And I saw how it was extinguished when the sickness flared up again. Twice she was operated on. Now she's lying out there, and in a few days she will hear the final decision. Perhaps she still hopes, and that is what is terrible. Once more I will see hope extinguished in her. And I can do nothing, because I have nothing to give. I no longer have faith. I have only my own helplessness.

"I've tried to pray, even though I know that it's meaningless. I don't believe, and I know that prayer is useless. Yet, I pray that she might find faith — is that not absurd? And I continue to pray, every hour of the day, while I follow her down the steps, rung by rung, down into darkness and emptiness. It is the only thing I can do."

"Why do I tell you all this?" He looked up. "I know that you can not help, either. I've told more to you than to any other human being — yes, more than I knew myself. Why?" Weary, he continued to stare at his hands. But then he looked up again, staring into space, as if a new, terrible suspicion rose up and became a certainty. "Perhaps that is why I tell you this. Because I want someone to be my witness."

When Olav Klungland returned home towards one in the morning, he let himself in quietly so that he would not awaken his family. He went directly up to his workroom, tore a sheet from the desk calendar and wrote, "He does not dare look the future in the eye because he has nothing to fight for: he no longer has a driving inspiration."

It was something he had realized on the way home in the taxi, and he had repeated it to himself, afraid that he would forget it. Now he felt relieved because he had written it down. It was as if he were on a lake in a leaky rowboat and managed to plug a rag into the crack.

When, a little later, he stood in the kitchen and found that there was still cognac left in the cupboard, he felt even more relieved. He took a stiff drink from the bottle before he made himself a highball. With the cognac and two bottles of seltzer he returned to his workroom. Vigdis was awake. She stood at the desk and read the note he had written.

"Excuse me. I thought it was a message. Is it about the minister?"

He nodded.

"How is he?"

Klungland, not trusting himself to discuss the matter, answered quickly, "A hell of a story. His daughter died from a drug overdose and his wife has cancer."

"Is she coping?"

"I don't know. It sounds pretty hopeless. He's going to call me tomorrow when he gets word from the hospital."

"It must be terrible," she said sympathetically. He knew she was not concerned about the minister. This was a situation that could strike them as well. She thought about the children, about him, about herself.

"I think we ought to have a thorough checkup. Both of us. And the children, too," she said after a moment. When he did not respond, she turned back to his note. "Will you write about it?"

"Write?"

"Since you've begun to take notes?"

"You think I'm like that? Am I the kind of person who cannot be interested in someone without writing about him?"

"I'm sorry.... Come, let's go to bed," she whispered. She was naked under the thin nightgown, and, moving the highball to avoid splashing her, he put his arm around her waist. He had a choice between two kinds of sedatives, but he could not decide.

"I'll come in a little while," he said at last.

He emptied the highball glass as soon as she was gone. Why had the minister's story disturbed him so? Was it the fate of the wife and the daughter? — And what, then, about the suffering that was taking place in Vietnam? The thought popped automatically into his head. The minister's fate was like a drop in the sea in comparison with the suffering that the Vietnamese experienced every moment, every hour of the day. But his thoughts about Vietnam made him uncomfortable, as if they were part of a process of self-deception. Vietnam did not bother him; nor the minister. It was he, himself, that concerned him and the days and the weeks that lay before him.

He thought about his unfinished speech, the conference in Stockholm on "The Responsibility of the Creative Artist," the novel that he would, in all likelihood, never complete. But what plagued him most was the certainty that in the midst of the aimless days that lay before him, he would return to questions that, he knew, had no answer — questions about death and about the true meaning of life.

He was tired of thinking about it and tired of talking about it. But precisely because he was tired of thinking about it, he had always felt an urgent need to talk about it. He was disgusted with himself when he recalled all those exalted and endless discussions about death.

The question always seemed to crop up: during parties or when they were alone at home. Most often he began the discussion. He felt relieved when someone died so he could begin to talk about it without seeming peculiar. In fact, it was foolish to discuss it, because there was, to be sure, only one answer — that we would die and that there was nothing we could do about it.

Nevertheless he continued to discuss death. When he grew overzealous, it was almost always late at night when he had been drinking, and he often noticed that Vigdis looked at him strangely and studied him. Sometimes she said, "Don't you think it's unusual that you're so obsessed with this subject?" He was irritated when she looked at him in that way. He felt that she "analyzed" him, and his bitterness about psychology and everything that it stood for, angered him. "Why shouldn't I talk about death? I write about it. It's my profession!" He always defended himself by evoking his profession. He was obsessed by death simply because it was interesting. When they came home from some gathering, she would, on occasion, reproach him. "You bore others with all this talk about death," she would say, especially when they had been visiting fellow members of the communist party.

But Klungland suspected that the party members were really more interested in the topic than they would admit. Sometimes, particularly during open discussions in which people participated who were members of other political parties or who belonged to no particular political faction, the question would suddenly arise — What is the meaning of life if everything ends in death? — something like that. The question was always distressing, and in the course of his twenty-five years in politics, he had always responded with the same answer: "We communists are not interested in the afterlife. Our task is to improve life for people here on earth." He always gave a similar reply, and his answer inevitably produced the same result: the issue was no longer discussed.

Now, when he thought about this pat response that he had so often rattled off, he was ashamed. It was a cliché. What good was life if the only thing we had to look forward to was annihilation? If life was a tunnel into which we were forced, a tunnel that ended in an abyss, what did anything matter?

When he was younger, he had had a romantic conception of his own death. He pictured himself, at one time or another in the distant future, melting into nature, becoming one with it. In this connection he always imagined a particular spot out in the archipelago, near where he had later built his vacation cabin. Perhaps that was why he had bought that specific lot.

But he had grown older, and wishful thinking no longer comforted him. With what in nature could his consciousness unite? With nothing. And nothing joined with nothing was nothing.

After he discovered politics, his notion of death changed. He would die in battle. Not in a literal sense, but in the certainty that the struggle was underway, the struggle for the liberation of humanity. He would die in solidarity with those other warriors. This notion, too, had its specific image. He saw himself surrounded by his loved ones. Vigdis and the children wept at his bedside, and while the final darkness descended, he heard himself whisper, "How are they doing at Monte Grosso?" — and Vigdis would whisper back, "They struggle. They are advancing!"

But this, too, was a wishful daydream. It was likely that the reality would be completely different. Realizing that, he began, at the same time, to think seriously of death as something that would happen to *him*. He would be annihilated. It was not merely a possibility. It was a certainty. Only the time that it would happen was uncertain.

It had to be acknowledged. The only honest attitude to take was to acknowledge his own death, to make it a part of his life. To write about it.

But one day he would no longer be able to write.

He studied the note on the table and the words he had written. And now he understood that what had most shaken him in the story was the minister's confession that he had lost his faith! He had realized that in the taxi.

Have I, too, lost my faith? Do I, myself, stand at the Carriage Stone? Am I no longer a believing communist? What is wrong with me?

He walked over to the desk and took out the manuscript for his speech, leafed through it until he found the section on hope. It was a denunciation of despondency and despair. "....This is precisely what the reactionaries desire — to sow hopelessness and despair. They want to smash hope because it is a threat to them. But never has hope been stronger than today. Everywhere people rise up against oppression. Everywhere in the world people struggle against humiliation, exploitation, and despair. The people will be victorious, and their victory is the hope of the world. The imperialists can attack, but they know that their time is over. They can whip the sea, but they can never stop the waves..."

The words disgusted him because there was no connection between them and his own doubts. What good is it to me if the revolution will be victorious, if I am dead — I! — and at once he recalled the minister's description of how he felt as he read through his old sermons.

Klungland lay the manuscript aside and brought his note pad forward. Quickly, so that he would not change his mind, he struck out the word "he" and wrote "I" in its place. Then he read the words that stood there — "I do not dare look the future in the eye because I have nothing to fight for; I no longer have a driving inspiration." He crumpled the page into a ball and threw it into the waste basket.

"Nonsense!" he said and regretted that he had not gone to bed with Vigdis. Now he could be sleeping in her arms.

He undressed and, naked, he crawled in beside her. But she slept. He caressed her body, and she murmured, half asleep, "I can't now. Why didn't you come sooner?" He continued to caress her, and she fell asleep again and began to snore. He rested his hand on her breast and realized that he was searching for something. Was there not a lump there that he had not felt before? He withdrew his hand. Perhaps it was *he* who would sit by her death bed? And once more he thought of the minister who now was waiting for the report from the hospital. Tomorrow Grøtteland would telephone. Perhaps the case was not really so hopeless. Perhaps the minister would call in the morning to report that his wife would have another operation. The doctors were so capable these days: they never gave up. As Klungland drifted into sleep, he comforted himself with that thought.

He did not rise until towards eleven, and once more he found himself at his desk, staring at Che Guevara's summons to begin work. But he could not concentrate. He waited for the minister's call.

While he waited, he leafed through the program for the conference in Stockholm on "The Responsibility of the Creative Artist." He could not tolerate the thought of all the speeches, the pleas, the words, the heated discussions in the afternoons and the wrangling in the evenings. He simply could not stand thinking about all that. Vigdis sounded worried when he telephoned her at noon and told her that he had decided not to go to Stockholm.

"I think you should reconsider before you cancel the tickets. Wait until tomorrow anyway!"

"I've made up my mind!" But, nevertheless, he listened to her suggestion and neglected to cancel the tickets. With his attention on the silent telephone he began to leaf through the manuscript of the novel that he now was certain he would not complete this year. It was a huge, confused pile of handwritten and typed pages, a chaos of notes, rough drafts, scribbled remarks. He found it painful to read through his first drafts: one recognized, with shame, one's helplessness. Now he wanted to throw everything out. Was there any sense at all in struggling for two years with a book that would, perhaps, be read by only a few? Why not stop writing and devote all his energies to politics? Sooner or later he had to choose.

While leafing at random through the papers, he came upon the yellowed newspaper clipping. There were close-ups of two faces, two old people — a man and a woman. This photograph had been the germ of the idea for the novel he was working on. It would be a book about the loneliness of people in a planned suburban development. Two years earlier he had read a notice in the paper and seen the picture of the couple. They were found drowned in the sea beyond Bygdø, but since it had been impossible for the police to make an identification, their photograph had been published. When they were later identified, it was learned that they were a married couple, two lonely people, who had sought death by drowning.

The story had moved Klungland, but he was never able to do anything with it. When he had worked on the material, it developed in a completely different direction. Now he studied the forgotten picture, and he noticed that something was kindled within him. He felt a fierce restlessness, similar to the anxiety he had experienced the time he had tried to quit smoking. He laid the picture aside and went down to the living room and out into the garden, but the weather was raw and cold and he immediately went back inside. When he crossed through the parlor on the way up to his study, he disconnected the telephone. He did not want to be disturbed just now.

Once more he studied the photograph. He took his pencil to make a note, but put it aside immediately. No, no, he thought. Take it easy. Not too fast. Just let it come of itself. Nothing on paper yet. He resisted the temptation each time he wanted to begin to take notes. It was like slapping an impatient child on the hand. Take it easy. Careful.

He stared at the two dead faces and felt something of what he had experienced when he saw the picture for the first time, that which he had seen in a flash, but had not been able to develop because he lacked an idea and because he lacked the language of the plot which was something completely different from words and sentences. Now it took shape. Now he saw it for himself. Now he could do it!

Restless, he roamed through the house occupying himself with practical tasks so that he would avoid beginning to write too soon. He straightened a picture, fastened a screw in a shelf, mounted shelving paper. He was glad that he had disconnected the telephone in time. He had to keep the minister at a distance.

Have I the right to use people in this way, he wondered, and he immediately answered that naturally he had that right. Where could he find his material if not in his own life? And if literature had any value, any use... Here he stopped because he knew he lied. He did not consider usefulness. Of course he could not avoid some guilt, but it was as thin as diluted fruit juice. The concentrated essence itself, that was the deep joy he felt because something was taking shape.

Grøtteland telephoned at about eight in the evening, and Klungland stood quietly by as Vigdis repeated his excuse. "Unfortunately, he had to attend an important meeting."

When the family had gone to bed, Klungland sat down at the desk and began to outline the plot. The story took an entirely different turn. The characters remained basically the same, but in the earlier version, they were contrived, artificial, fabricated. He had not known them. Now he knew them; now he could use their own voice, and he could lead them where he wanted. It was exhausting work. He did not dare let his imagination lead him astray. It was like steering a river boat caught in a heavy current. But at the same time he felt great peace, because he knew his destination. He had a driving inspiration.

Everything went well and he felt no fatigue. Vigdis and the children slept. While he wrote he felt a remarkable sense of power, of mastery over fate, as if he were lord of life and death.

He did not finish until almost four in the morning. The rough outline of the action was clear. He had followed the wanderings of two lonely people towards the final shore. As Klungland undressed, he paused and studied Vigdis. She lay on her back and slept with her mouth half open. The soft light of the lamp threw shadows across her face, deepening her eye sockets, her temples, the hollow under her jaw. He felt somehow ashamed to stare at her while she lay there defenseless. But he did not turn away. The minister's wife must look like that, he thought. Perhaps she lay like that this very moment.

He had never met Grøtteland's wife and probably never would. Nevertheless he knew how she looked.

But, as it turned out, he was mistaken. He was to meet her.

His trip was once more on his schedule. The following morning, as they sat at the breakfast table, Klungland said to his wife, "I've thought carefully about it. I'm going to follow your advice."

"I think that's a wise decision. You'll meet a good many interesting people in Stockholm."

He realized that she was relieved. "That's exactly what I was thinking," he answered, meekly.

The conference was supposed to begin the next day, but Klungland decided to leave immediately. He longed for streets filled with strangers and for an anonymous hotel room. He looked forward to three long conference days when he could be alone, pretending to listen to the discussions. Never was one so blessedly alone as at such a conference. The plane would not depart until noon, but he had Vigdis drive him into the city on her way to work in the morning. He wanted to be quits with the house so that nothing could interfere with his departure.

For two hours he sat in a cafe near the bus terminal. He smoked, read newspapers and waited for the bus that would drive him to the airport. All the while he felt an uneasiness, as if something would interfere with his journey, something would prevent him from leaving. Only after he had checked his baggage and stood in the departure line did he relax.

And then, glancing back one final time, he saw the minister. Grøtteland crossed the hall, a woman leaning on his arm. That had to be his wife. When Klungland turned back to the line, he thought, "They've been given notice. She's going home to die."

It was his turn to show his ticket, but he hesitated, indecisive. The man behind nudged him. "Excuse me, but it's your turn." "I'm sorry," Klungland responded and let the man pass. Then he raced back across the hall. Grøtteland and his wife were nearing the exit now. They shuffled along slowly; it was obvious that the woman experienced pain when she walked. He remembered that the minister had said that when they went hiking she had always followed behind him. "Grøtteland!"

Klungland shouted, but they continued. They were at the door and he called again; not until he was directly behind them did they stop.

When the minister turned, he did not seem to recognize Klungland at first. Grøtteland seemed confused and stared at him as if he were a stranger or as if they had met only after a long absence. "This is my wife," he said at last. "Elna, here is someone who would like to meet you!"

She turned.

"Oh!" he cried in dismay. Only later did he think about how tactless his reaction was and how she must have felt about it. He could not understand why he reacted so badly. Was it because he saw before him, once more, the expression in the eyes of Heimdal, his political associate? Something overwhelmed him, something that had been pursuing him and that now overtook him. What was it? He took the hand that she hesitantly held out to him. It was ice cold. He knew that his eyes were filled with tears, but he could not hold them back.

"Forgive me," he murmured and fled. The meeting had lasted less than a minute. He was still bewildered when, later, he found himself in the plane, listening to the whine of the engine. He had no idea why he had reacted like that, and his confusion only increased the fear that flooded over him as the plane broke through the thick cloud cover. The plane seemed to hover, motionless, in vast space, and even if he knew that it was illusion, it seemed to him that he had begun an endless journey from which he would never return. When they landed in Stockholm an hour later, this feeling was replaced by a sense of crushing loneliness. He thought of Vigdis, the children, his home — they seemed light years away.

The hotel was fully occupied when he arrived — he was there a day early — but in the course of the evening a room would, perhaps, become available. For hours he wandered aimlessly through the city. He searched out the busiest streets, let himself flow with the stream, stopped before showcases, read the theater placards. While he walked he tried to reason with himself.

He was back at the hotel by eight. The first delegates to the conference had arrived, but Klungland avoided them. He told the receptionist that he had to leave immediately. He caught the last flight back to Oslo, and towards one in the morning his taxi pulled up outside his home.

They left for their cottage the next day. They had planned to wait until the day before Palm Sunday, but Vigdis insisted that they drive there immediately. "I don't want you to be alone for three days and become despondent." Her tone told him she would not change her mind. Nor did he object. Within a few hours she had arranged things: taken time off from the institute, spoken with the school, packed. That very same evening they sat in their motorboat and watched the sunset, she astern, at the tiller, and he and the children shifting to hold the fishing lines. In the gathering dusk the pollack began to bite.

They were there for ten days. They were together the entire time. Never before had they been so close. They planted vegetables and flowers, went hiking, fished. In the evening they sat by the fireplace, drinks in hand. They made love every single night. His experience seemed distant, more remote with each passing day. But when they would stroll down to the boathouse or sit on a rock and watch the children fishing out in the sound, it could suddenly envelop him like the breath of a chill wind: "So long as it lasts." — And at once he was within another, invisible, reality which he, nevertheless, sensed was more true than that he now experienced. He watched her in the cottage, there among the rocks, or in the lemon yellow rowboat with the children in their orange life jackets. Something was still wrong.

"What are you thinking about?" she would ask.

They returned home on the Tuesday after Easter.

When out driving, they would often sing camp songs, popular ballads, and hymns. They had sung during the trip down to the coast. Now he drove in silence. Despair overwhelmed him to such a degree that he could not bring himself to sing.

"Do you worry about returning to the city?"

"That, too."

"After all, that's where we live."

"Yes, I know damn well it's where we live, but what will we live off if I can't write!" he cried. "I don't earn anything from politics. That's been nothing but an expense."

He grew more and more bitter the nearer they came to the city, and he began to complain about how he had been used. He had been politically active for almost a lifetime. Often he had been occupied for months on end with campaigns and talks and articles while his own work had to wait.

"What have I actually gotten in return for all that? Not one single øre. Once they gave me a bottle of whiskey for an article. They take me for granted." He fell silent.

"But was that why you did it?"

"Why I did it?"

"For money?"

"Of course it wasn't that."

"Then what didn't you get in return? Recognition? Praise?"

"Shut up!" He reacted angrily, but he had to admit that her question had some validity.

"Yes, recognition. That, too," he admitted. "But when it comes down to it, I was just used. They make all the decisions."

"You want to be included in the decision-making as well?"

Her question only upset him more, and she pointed to the dial on the speedometer. It neared a hundred. He eased up on the gas, but within moments the speed began to climb again.

"This pack of opportunists. These so-called radicals who are now combining forces," he cried. "They're so pseudo-elegant that they won't have anything to do with us old-fashioned communists. Just wait until they're successful and the coalition is a reality. Then what do you think will happen...."

"Why don't you, yourself, join in the negotiations?"

"Because I want to write, damn it!" he cried.

He realized that his anger was an evasion. He did not want to tie himself down, to assume responsibility. He did not want anything different. Did he want something to live on or something to live for? Was it a simple choice between writing and politics? And was that not, as well, self-deception? He knew that the choice was over something more elemental.

When they arrived home, towards eight, he went directly to his study. He despaired. "Things cannot go on like this," he thought. "We cannot race off to the cottage every time I become despondent."

Vigdis called to him from outside in the garden, and he went to the window. She was working in the flower bed. "She is all I have," he thought. "She can be a nag, but I have no one else." He thought about the minister and the meeting out by the airport and about how foolishly he had behaved, and suddenly fear, once more, overwhelmed him. Had he not felt a lump in her left breast?

She glanced up and waved, and when he came down she joined him, praising the newly panelled house.

"Tomorrow I think you should begin to paint it."

"Do you think so?"

"It might rot."

"Rot?" She did not understand carpentry, but perhaps she understood him. He had considered painting the house, but had dismissed the idea.

"I have to get back to my writing," he said uncertainly.

"Yes, certainly, but it has to be painted. It's worth the effort."

He eagerly grasped the suggestion. In the evening they discussed colors and agreed on a muted rose with blue trim. Early the next morning he was at the paint store, and when she came home in the afternoon he had almost finished the first wall of the house. She went right to work on the windows.

They were at it for a week, painting until late into the night. That was the week the first delicate leaves appeared on the birches and the cherry trees burst into bloom. When, during the evening of the 30th of April, they stood together and admired the house, its new coat of paint shimmering in the twilight, he thought, "Now I am utterly content."

He was not even worried about the talk that he was to give the next afternoon, on May Day. He had not tried to finish it, but had taken out an old speech — one he had delivered six years earlier. To his surprise, he discovered that he could use it almost without changing a word. In fact, it was more relevant now than when he gave it the first time.

During the flight to Kristiansand, Olav Klungland read through his speech a final time. He had to smile when he thought about the furor it had once created. It was first delivered during an Anti-Vietnam demonstration, and instead of talking about Vietnam, he had discussed Norway's own struggle and the necessity for solidarity. Afterwards he was criticized because he had addressed such a controversial issue. Indeed, some had even accused him of intentionally fomenting discord. No one would react like that today.

Two hours later, in high spirits, he stood at the flag-draped podium, aware that his speech captured the rapt attention of the crowd. When he noticed the minister on the edge of the gathering, Klungland thought to himself, "I am unchanged. My principles are the same. I stand on the firm foundation of class struggle."

After the lengthy applause and the singing of the "Internationale," many came up and thanked him. An old party comrade winked and whispered: "I heard it six years ago, but it was better today."

The plane would leave in two hours, but before that, a small reception was planned at the home of a party member. They would have some lunch and drink a toast in honor of the occasion. As they made their way to the waiting car, Klungland hoped that the minister was gone. But before they reached the car someone called his name, and when Klungland turned, the minister stood there waiting. Klungland realized immediately that something had changed. Grøtteland seemed calm as he reached out his hand.

"Good to see you again," Klungland said and asked quickly, to get it over with, "How is your wife doing?"

"She's dead."

"It happened so quickly?"

The minister glanced over to the car where Klungland's associates waited. "It would have been nice to talk for a while, but I see that you're busy."

"I'm rather busy."

"I understand perfectly," the minister said, and again he offered his hand. "I just wanted to drive over and say hello. And give you her greeting. That was, as a matter of fact, one of the last things she asked of me."

"Wait a bit..."

As Klungland walked over to the car he thought, "Why am I doing this? It really is unnecessary."

"I'm so sorry," he told his associates, and nodded in the direction of the minister. "He's just lost his wife, and he wants to talk to me."

They were true and faithful comrades. They understood. No one complained; no one pressed him. He watched them as they drove off.

Klungland and Grøtteland exchanged only a few words as they drove into the city. The minister mentioned that his wife had been buried the day before.

"I hope she didn't suffer...." Klungland was about to say "too much," but he stopped himself.

"She died in her sleep. In the end her heart gave out."

During the drive Klungland thought about the minister's despair the last time they had been together. Something was not right. Was Grøtteland, purely and simply, relieved because it was over?

The minister lived in a modern apartment in the city, and as soon as they entered it, he asked if Klungland was hungry. "I have plenty of sandwiches in the refrigerator. Left over from the funeral."

"I'm not hungry."

"Beer or coffee? Or perhaps white wine?"

"Coffee," Klungland responded curtly as he went into the parlor. He is purely and simply relieved, he thought. There is nothing more to it than that. He had to light a cigarette to quiet himself. Bouquets of flowers were everywhere. The air was saturated with their heavy perfume. On the coffee table lay a photograph album, and he began to leaf through it. Most of the pictures were of the daughter, Lillian, as a baby, a youngster, and an adult — the last must have been taken a short time before she died. She was a sweet, ordinary girl. The pictures did not impress him. Not so the photographs of Grøtteland's wife, Elna. What the minister had said was apparently true. She must have been beautiful. One of the photos was taken during their stay in Finnmark. She stood on the deck of a fishing boat, the sea in the background, holding up a wriggling cod. Her face was young and strong and full of laughter. Did she ever really look like that, Klungland thought uneasily, and he remembered that during the Easter vacation he had taken a similar photograph of Vigdis. The film had not yet been developed.

"Yes, and this one is Hausebakken," the minister mentioned, pulling up a chair on the opposite side of the table.

The farm was different than Klungland had imagined, wider and more open. "I gathered that," Klungland answered rather coolly, and lay the album aside.

The minister took it up immediately and continued to study the photograph. "I'm going there in a few days. The people who bought it were at the funeral, and they said that I could stay until the summer vacation. I have temporary leave."

Perhaps Grøtteland recognized Klungland's irritation, because he added quickly, as if he wanted to compensate for what he had just said, "Naturally it's painful to think that she is gone and that she won't experience it." He glanced across the room, and his eyes rested upon one of the bouquets of flowers. "Nevertheless, I'm grateful for the days we had together before she died."

"But she's dead!" Klungland responded with brutal frankness. Grøtteland's peacefulness made him increasingly angry. The man seemed so absolutely content.

"Yes, she's dead. But I believe that we'll meet again. That's why I'm happy in the midst of my sorrow and loss."

"You mean that you've found your faith again?"

"I've found, once more, that which I'd lost," the minister answered hesitantly. "Faith, hope...."

"And love!" He sounded ironic, and he meant it that way.

"Yes, love. That was the worst to lose."

"And all this you've found again because she died? Wasn't that somewhat costly? For her?"

"No, no, it wasn't because she died."

Klungland was so angry that he wanted to get up and leave. "What was it then that happened?"

From the way the minister stared helplessly into space, it was obvious that he was aware of Klungland's anger. At last he said, "What happened? We met you."

The coffee pot boiled over in the kitchen and the minister ran off. Klungland listened to the clinking of the cups in the other room and he looked at the clock. If he caught a taxi, he could reach his associates before they sat down to lunch, and he would still make his plane.

But when the minister came in with the tray, Klungland did not rise. He said quickly, before Grøtteland had finished pouring, "I remember that we met there at the airport, but that was accidental. I was supposed to leave the next day, but I changed my mind...." He was about to say, "Because I could not bring myself to talk to you," but he thought that was too impolite.

The minister looked at him, astonished. "You changed your mind?"

"I had to get away. I was about to..." He was fast losing his enthusiasm, and he thought, I can still get to the luncheon in time if I take a cab.

"I called you the evening before, as I promised," the minister said after a while. "I was relieved when I heard that you were out. You were at a meeting?"

Klungland did not answer.

"Yes, I promised to telephone, but I believe I would not have been able to talk to you. Just before, the doctors had delivered their verdict. Their final verdict. There was nothing to be done. We could go home. It could be a matter of days or weeks..."

The minister was silent. It was difficult for him to continue. "That's how it was," he said, fumbling. "That's how it was," he repeated. "Some time during the night I made my decision. I knew it was the only way out. I had reached the final rung on the ladder and I knew I could not turn back. I had to follow her down the next step. I could not live without her.

"In the morning I met her at the hospital at the appointed time. She was weak and it was all she could do to walk from the taxi into the airport terminal. I, too, was dead tired. I thought of the plane trip, of the waiting apartment, of the days that lay before us and of my own helplessness. I had only one profound desire — to lie beside her and sleep and sleep and sleep. We sat on a bench in the hall and waited. We did not look at each other, but I remember that I held her hand and that with the other I clutched, in my pocket, the pill box. I stared at the suitcases in front of me, and I heard myself say, 'We'll go back to the hotel. We'll sleep!'

"And only then did I dare look at her. For a long time we studied each other. She nodded, and we rose and walked towards the exit. Then you came. I heard you call me, and I thought that we would get away before you reached us. But you came running after us. Why did you do that?"

Olav Klungland had difficulty making his voice seem natural when he finally answered, "I don't know."

"That was what I said when we were in the taxi and Elna asked about you. We sat in the cab without speaking, without touching, and we had almost reached the hotel before she took my hand and asked, 'Why did he do that? Why did he call us?' And I answered that I did not know.

"No, I do not know. I do not understand what happened. I remember nothing except the incomprehensible joy that flooded over me when I asked her if, perhaps, we should return to the airport, and I heard her whisper, 'Yes'. She rested her head on my shoulder and began to cry. 'I want to go home,' she said.

"We drove back to the airport, close in the arms of each other, as we had lain in the prow of the motorboat that summer night we first loved each other. How did it happen? I cannot explain. It was so undeserved. We had seven days together, seven days of such happiness as I had not thought possible. If that happiness could have been weighed and counted, it would have been enough for a long life, for all of our long and lonely life. All the bad that had existed between us was no more. So long as I live I shall thank God for the days we had together and for the happiness I feel, now, when I think of her, my beloved. Only one word is magnificent enough — thanks."

Grøtteland left the room, but he returned a moment later.

"When I think about my life, I realize that everything was poisoned by my fear of death. It killed every chance for happiness and made me, myself, evil. But the evil I did to others no longer oppresses me. Perhaps I could not have done otherwise. And, in any case, it was all, possibly, not without meaning. I only know that now death has given meaning to my life. Oh God, I am happy again!"

For a long time Grøtteland seemed completely pre-occupied. Klungland almost thought he had been forgotten. "Will you serve as a minister again?" he asked at last.

"Minister? What good would that do? To begin all over with sermons, to struggle with words and sentences? I don't even know what I would say." Grotteland seemed lost in thought. "I am no minister. I cannot teach others what I have not learned myself. When I look back on my life and wonder what I have learned, the answer is always the same: nothing. I have learned nothing — except one thing: that I know nothing, understand nothing, that all that I have received has been undeserved, a gift of grace. No, I don't know what I'll do. It's possible that I'll continue teaching in the school. Perhaps I can be of use. Perhaps I can finally represent something for others."

The time neared for Klungland's return flight to Oslo, and the minister said he would drive his guest out to the airport. Klungland, restlessly pacing the parlor, waited for the minister to clear the table and get ready. The shelves in the room were filled with books, and he glanced over the titles. There stood his own novels. As far as he could see every one of them was there. The last one, as well. He took it from the shelf and read the greeting he had written. When he tried to leaf through it, he discovered that some of the pages were not cut, and he quickly placed it back on the shelf.

A band was playing outside, and he walked over to the window. The main parade must be over. A truck with banners drove by. I am the same and my thinking has not changed, he told himself after the music faded. But something was different. He thought about the years that lay ahead of him, and of tomorrow. Possibly, in the morning, he would begin giving the house a second coat of paint. In a week he and Vigdis would stand back and admire his work and he would think, "I am content!" And then, once more, the old anxiety would return. He thought about the May Day speeches he would deliver in the future, and about the vacations at the cottage, the fishing trips on the bay. Would the discontent, that he had always resisted, pursue him still?

Would it never end, he wondered fearfully.

It had begun to rain, and when he sat in the plane, he could barely discern the minister waiting over by the hanger. Then the plane taxied out to the runway, and Grøtteland disappeared in the mist.

Just as the plane took off, Klungland felt a fresh wave of despair — a restless anxiety because in returning to security he feared that it would become his life, this complacent security that he had always yearned for. He knew that it was an illusion.

As the plane rose up into darkness, Klungland felt a desperate need to give some tangible and physical expression to that which now possessed him. With all his strength he pressed against the seat belt and stared at the window pane. Suddenly the plane broke out of the clouds and continued its climb. He leaned forward, looking out over infinite, sunlit space. In the far distance a pillar of cloud towered up against the pale blue sky. He fastened his gaze on it, and softly, so that no one would hear, he whispered, "Take not this restlessness from me."

mP .

Please re
Dychweler erb

Born and raised on the Wirral Peninsula in England, **Charlotte Hawkes** is mum to two intrepid boys who love her to play building block games with them and who object loudly to the amount of time she spends on the computer. When she isn't writing—or building with blocks—she is company director for a small Anglo/French construction firm. Charlotte loves to hear from readers, and you can contact her at her website: charlotte-hawkes.com.

Also by Charlotte Hawkes

The Army Doc's Secret Wife
The Surgeon's Baby Surprise
A Bride to Redeem Him
The Surgeon's One-Night Baby
Christmas with Her Bodyguard
A Surgeon for the Single Mum

Hot Army Docs miniseries

Encounter with a Commanding Officer
Tempted by Dr Off-Limits

Discover more at millsandboon.co.uk.